## "Marry

Olivia could almost hear her own words echoing. *Marry me. Marry me.*

"Marry you?" Guy repeated softly. He was standing very close, the impression of leashed power almost overwhelming.

"Yes." Olivia cleared her throat. "The only way I can get a residency permit is to marry an Australian. It would be strictly a business arrangement—just a formality, really." She risked a glance at his inscrutable face. "For David's sake...." she finished lamely.

There was a long pause. "You're willing to do this for David?" he asked at last. "Give up your career? Live in the outback? Marry a man you hardly know?"

"Yes."

There was another silence until, still looking out at the stockyards, he said, "All right, I'll marry you— on two conditions."

**Jessica Hart** was born in Ghana, but grew up in an Oxfordshire village. Her father was a civil engineer working overseas, so by the time she left school, she'd been to East Africa, South Africa, Papua New Guinea and Oman—and had acquired incurably itchy feet. After spending a year in New Zealand with a cousin, where she says she learned a thousand things to do with mutton, she studied French literature at Edinburgh University, graduating in 1981. Since then, she's had a haphazard series of jobs—production assistant at a theater, research assistant, waitress, teaching English, cook on an outback property—in England, Egypt, Kenya, Jakarta and Australia, respectively. She's also worked with Operation Raleigh, selecting Venturers for expeditions, which took her to Cameroon and Algeria. At present, she works as foreign news-desk secretary at the *Observer,* but eventually, she wants to leave London and take a further degree in Medieval History.

## Books by Jessica Hart

HARLEQUIN ROMANCE
3213—THE TROUBLE WITH LOVE

# WOMAN AT WILLAGONG CREEK
## Jessica Hart

## *Harlequin Books*

TORONTO • NEW YORK • LONDON
AMSTERDAM • PARIS • SYDNEY • HAMBURG
STOCKHOLM • ATHENS • TOKYO • MILAN
MADRID • WARSAW • BUDAPEST • AUCKLAND

Original hardcover edition published in 1992
by Mills & Boon Limited

ISBN 0-373-03231-5

Harlequin Romance first edition November 1992

WOMAN AT WILLAGONG CREEK

Printed in U.S.A.

# CHAPTER ONE

TYPICAL outback type, Olivia thought dispassionately, watching the man lean forward and speak to the hotel receptionist. There seemed to be plenty of them in Townsville; lean, brown, quiet-looking men in cattlemen's hats, somehow out of place in the bright holiday atmosphere.

She glanced at her watch again. Where *were* they? She had been sitting in the hotel foyer for two hours now, waiting out for a man and a boy. It had been over three years since she had seen David, but she was sure she would recognise him from the photos Diane had sent to England. And Guy Richardson would probably look very much like the man over there. Diane had mentioned him, of course. He was Pete's cousin, owner of some vast, ramshackle property in north-west Queensland. She seemed to remember hearing that he was a bachelor. No doubt he'd be more than relieved to get rid of the responsibility of a small boy.

Olivia's thoughts broke off as she saw the receptionist point in her direction. The man straightened and turned to look across at her. He had dark eyes and a direct, penetrating gaze, and for no reason Olivia felt her heart give an odd little leap. Suddenly he didn't look quite so typical.

He was heading towards her. There was a kind of controlled power about the way he moved, an assurance in the way he held himself, that made Olivia, normally the most confident of women, feel suddenly at a disadvantage.

He took off his hat, revealing dark brown hair cut close to his head. Olivia was unsurprised. She could tell already that curls or romantic stray locks of hair would not be this man's style.

'Olivia Bridewell?' His voice was deep, unhurried. 'I'm Guy Richardson.' He wasn't all that much taller than she was, Olivia realised when he stood in front of her, but the impression of contained strength was very strong. His face was angular, each plane distinct, with dark brows, a strong nose and a stubborn jaw. Not a remarkable-looking man by any means, but a man with presence, a man whose eyes and whose firm, inflexible mouth hinted at a character denied by his detached expression.

Olivia pulled herself together. 'Hello,' she smiled, holding out her hand.

She was taken aback when Guy Richardson didn't return her smile. He merely clasped her hand briefly and then dropped it, as if it were something unpleasant.

Perhaps he was shy?

He didn't look shy. He looked tough, capable, self-possessed. There was an air of stillness about him that made Olivia nervous. She was used to the more frenetic activity of the arts world.

'Um...where's David?' she asked, keeping the bright smile pinned to her face.

'At Willagong Creek.'

'But didn't you get my letter?' Olivia looked at him blankly. It had been over a month since she had written saying when she would arrive in Australia to take over her responsibilities as David's guardian.

'I wouldn't be here if I hadn't had it. You told me to meet you here this morning.' Guy sat down on the chair opposite her and looked her over with unfathomable deep dark brown eyes. Outback eyes, very creased at the edges from years of squinting at far horizons; they travelled over her slowly, taking in the long blue-green eyes, the flawless features and the unstudied elegance of her thinly striped grey and white suit. 'Here I am.'

She felt her temper rising. She was not used to being looked over as if she were a cow! 'Perhaps you could explain?' she said coldly. 'I was expecting to see David too. I've come a long way to collect him.'

'He's not a parcel, Miss Bridewell,' said Guy. 'He's a kid who only lost his parents a couple of months ago. I left him behind deliberately. I don't think he's ready to be *collected*.'

Olivia flushed at his tone. 'I didn't mean it like that,' she admitted, realising how unfeeling she must have sounded. 'I was just anxious to see him again.'

'So anxious that you waited two months before you could be bothered to come out to Australia?'

She set her teeth. 'I was on tour with the orchestra in Japan when Diane and Pete were killed,' she said, as calmly as she could. 'I explained all that in my letter. I didn't even see the letter from the lawyer until I got home three weeks later.' She paused, remembering that awful day, the shock of reading about her dearest friend's death in stark, undeniable print. Even now it was hard to believe. Taking a deep breath, she went on, 'I came as quickly as I could, but I had to sort out my job and my flat...it takes time.' She hoped she sounded reasonable. Guy Richardson seemed to have put her on the defensive. 'Anyway, I'm here now.' She tried another smile, one that normally had men turning handsprings, but Guy was unmoved.

He laid his hat on the table between them. In jeans and brown checked shirt, he looked as if he had stepped out of a Western, but there was an implacability about him that made Olivia wary of dismissing him as a mere cowboy.

'What had you planned to do with David?' he asked.

*Had* planned? She raised an eyebrow. 'I can stay six months on my visa, but I can't really afford to be away that long. I thought we'd spend some time getting to know each other here, and then we'll have to go back to London.'

'I see. And what if I don't agree to that?'

*'Don't agree?'* Olivia repeated incredulously. 'I don't think it's a question of your agreeing. *I* am David's legal guardian, not you.'

'It's not quite as simple as that,' Guy said, an edge to his voice. 'You weren't around when you were needed. There wasn't anyone else, so I took

David back to Willagong Creek with me. He's settled down now, and he's as happy as he can be under the circumstances. How do you think he's going to feel about being up-rooted again and dragged off to a strange country with a strange woman? No, Miss Bridewell, I'm not just going to hand him over to you now that you've bothered to turn up, legal guardian or no legal guardian.'

Olivia had remarkable eyes. Tropical-sea eyes, Diane had always described them enviously, more than blue and less than green. Like the sea, their colour was changeable, and now they narrowed angrily to the cool clear green of the shallows.

'I don't care for your attitude, Mr Richardson,' she said cuttingly. 'It's not a question of *bothering* to turn up. I've been arranging my affairs so that I can take care of David properly. That's meant letting my flat and resigning from my job, so that I can spend time out here with him before "dragging him off to a strange country", as you call it. That seemed to me to be the responsible thing to do, instead of rushing out here and having to go back to England to sort things out straight away. That would have been even more unsettling for David, surely?

'Furthermore, I am not a *strange woman*. I was Diane's closest friend, and she obviously trusted me to bring up her son as she wanted. I'm grateful to you for looking after David, but I have no intention of ignoring my responsibilities at your say-so!'

Olivia had a formidable reputation at work for her ability to cut people down to size, but Guy Richardson was unimpressed. 'Surely your responsibility is to do what's best for David?'

'Of course it is. At last we agree!'

'It would be best for David to stay with me,' Guy said calmly.

Olivia shook back her curtain of shining hair. 'It's out of the question!'

'Why?'

'You can't look after him properly, for a start.'

'I've looked after him for the last two months while you were sorting out your career,' he pointed out.

She frowned. 'That was a temporary measure. David's only eight. He needs a woman to look after him. It might be different if you were married.'

Guy shrugged. 'I'm going to get a housekeeper anyway.'

'I hardly think a housekeeper will be able to provide the love and attention that a little boy needs!' Olivia snapped. 'I'm sorry, but it's just not on. You're obviously fond of David, but even you must see that the outback is no place to bring up a child.'

'It didn't do me any harm,' he pointed out. 'Or David's father. Have you ever been to the outback, Miss Bridewell?'

She hesitated. 'No... but I can imagine what it's like, stuck out in the middle of nowhere. David needs to go to school, quite apart from anything else. Diane wouldn't have wanted him to run wild.'

'We're not savages!' Guy's voice was cold. 'David can do School of the Air until he's old enough to go to boarding-school.' He paused. 'Don't you think a child's lucky to have the chance to run wild nowadays? He wouldn't have much chance to do that in London, would he?'

'No, but he'd have other children to play with. He'd have cinemas and museums and funfairs. It's not so awful growing up in London.' She glanced at him, imitating his slow drawl. 'It didn't do me any harm.'

Guy looked at her, and under his dark gaze she felt herself grow suddenly hot, but he said only, 'We've talked about how I can't look after him properly. What about you?'

'Me?'

'You're the great career woman, aren't you?' he said, disparagingly. 'Diane was always talking about how successful you were. Olivia's in New York, Olivia's in Paris, Olivia's in Tokyo... When's Olivia going to be at home with David?'

'I've decided to go freelance,' she said loftily, determined to prove to him that she had thought everything through. 'I'll still have to do some travelling, but not as much, and I'll be able to work from home.'

'I thought you played in an orchestra?' Guy said. 'How are you going to do that from home?'

'I'm not a musician—I wish I were.' Olivia was a little surprised that Guy knew so much about her. 'I'm an administrator. I set up the tours with the promoters, make all the travel arrangements, deal with the bureaucracy, that kind of thing. It's not quite as glamorous as playing, but it's what I'm best at. Now that I've got my contacts, I don't need to work for a company any more.'

She paused. Useless to try and explain to this man the intimate, gossipy, often incestuous arts world, where professional relationships could be as fraught as personal ones, and when the two combined, as they had in the case of her and Tim, the result was frequently disastrous. If she was honest, she would have to admit that her decision to make the break from Hughes Mackenzie had as much to do with the break-up with Tim as with David or the desire to further her career, but she had no intention of telling that to Guy.

'I'd been thinking about going freelance for some time, actually,' she said instead. 'I was getting pretty tired of travelling so much. I suppose having David to think about gave me the incentive to make the break.'

'In fact, it's fitting in with your career plans?' Guy said bitingly.

Olivia's face froze. 'I wouldn't describe Diane and Pete's death like that.'

'Staying in London doesn't necessarily mean you'll be at home, though, does it?' he pointed out. 'I thought you were the type that was out at night-clubs every night with a different man. Having a kid around would cramp your style a bit, wouldn't it?'

Olivia had certainly had a full social life, but it was nothing like the debauched lifestyle Guy clearly imagined. 'I'm touched by your concern,' she said in a glacial voice, 'but I don't see that my social life is any of your business.' She was damned if she was going to start justifying herself to Guy Richardson!

There was a hostile pause. She stared at him in frustration. None of this was going as she had planned. She had thought she knew how to deal with men, but Guy Richardson had her baffled. He was unimpressed by her looks, impervious to her arguments.

Her eyes rested on him. He looked pretty ordinary, really—brown hair, deep brown eyes, skin deeply tanned from a lifetime in the sun. Certainly not her type. She liked witty, charming men who flirted and flattered, not this cool self-containment. Guy Richardson was not a man who would give anything away, she thought, eyeing the lean, uncompromising lines of his face. Why was he so keen to keep David? she wondered. Perhaps he wasn't as remote and unfeeling as he appeared. Unconsciously, her gaze travelled to his mouth and lingered there. What would he look like when he smiled?

Unaccountably, she shivered. Dragging her eyes away, she forced her mind back to the business in hand. 'Look,' she said, trying to sound coolly professional, 'we don't seem to be getting very far. You don't think I can look after David properly, and I don't think you can. Frankly, neither of us is ideal. You're a bachelor, with a property to run. I've got a career to think about. I also have a legal obligation to take care of David. I'd rather settle this amicably, but I suspect that, if it came to it, the courts would be on my side.'

She recoiled slightly as Guy leant forward until their faces were very close, his eyes dark with anger. The impression of suppressed power was very strong, and Olivia found that her heart was beating uncomfortably. 'Let's not start bandying threats around,' he said. His voice was quiet, but she edged further back into her seat. 'You may be used to pushing people around, but I'm not impressed by you or those big, beautiful eyes of yours, and you're not in an office now. We're talking about a little boy's life, not some business deal.' To her relief, he sat back. 'I suggest you come out to Willagong Creek with me tonight and see David for yourself. You might even consider asking him what *he* wants to do.'

She flushed, furious with herself for allowing him to intimidate her just then. 'David's too small to know what's best for him,' she said sharply.

'You're the one who wanted to settle this amicably,' he reminded her unpleasantly. 'All I'm asking is that you come to Willagong Creek with an open mind.' He paused. 'You might find it rather difficult to see David otherwise.'

Olivia glared at him. His meaning was quite clear. As far as he was concerned, David was safely tucked away in the outback, and she would have no idea how to go about finding him. 'I thought we weren't threatening each other,' she said, lifting her chin and meeting his eyes bravely.

'I'm not threatening you.' He returned her gaze blandly. 'I'm merely inviting you to visit us.'

Stifling the sharp retort that sprang to her lips, Olivia bent her head and stared at her hands, clasped together to stop them shaking with angry frustration. Her hair swung forward in a smooth fall of gold. It glinted in the light through the window and hid her expression.

Suddenly she felt very tired. She was still suffering from the effects of the long flight from London, and she hadn't bargained on such a hostile reception. A tide of resentment washed over her. It wasn't as if she had ever wanted children. She had her job, and, until a couple of months ago, she had had Tim. She hadn't wanted anything else.

Their relationship had dragged on for years, with neither of them prepared to commit themselves to marriage at the same time. Olivia had been as guilty as Tim of putting career first, and she was unprepared for the gap he had left in her life when he quite suddenly announced that he was going to marry someone else. She was unprepared too for the humiliation. They'd still had to work together, meet at the same parties, and in many ways her guardianship of David had allowed her an honourable escape to Australia for a few months.

She would have come anyway, Olivia told herself hastily. Diane had been the dearest of friends, and she was resolved to do her utmost for David—and that didn't include abandoning him to the outback and the unsmiling man sitting opposite her. Once she had made up her mind, Olivia could be stubborn, and she was not prepared to throw up all the practical arrangements she had made to care for David in the best way possible just because of one man's opposition.

Still, it was stupid to have allowed Guy to rile her. There was no point in things getting out of hand. The best thing to do was to go with him to Whatever-it-was Creek. She wouldn't change her mind, but at least she would see David, and perhaps they would be able to talk more reasonably...

'All right,' she said, coming to a reluctant decision. She lifted her head and faced Guy squarely, a hint of challenge in eyes which had deepened back to an intense blue. 'Thank you. I'd like to come.'

'Is this it?' Olivia climbed awkwardly out of the plane in her tight skirt and manoeuvred herself gingerly to the ground. Looking around, she could see nothing except scrubby gum-trees, a few tussocks of dry grass and red earth. And flies. They buzzed excitedly about her face, and she waved them away in disgust.

'This is it,' Guy confirmed, swinging himself easily down off the plane's wing. He glanced at Olivia, standing straight and slender in the sunlight, dressed in an absurdly inappropriate cream linen skirt and an olive-green silk top, appalled fascination writ large upon her face. His gaze took in the matching green high-heeled shoes, the linen jacket slung over one shoulder. Wear something comfortable to travel in, he had said. He sighed.

'Welcome to Willagong Creek.'

'But where's the house?' Olivia was finding it hard to believe that anyone would choose to live out here.

'The homestead's a couple of miles away.' Guy nodded his head at a dilapidated-looking vehicle which stood in the shade of a gum. 'We'll go in the ute.' He cast a disparaging glance at her shoes. 'Lucky for you we don't have to walk!'

Olivia merely gave him a cool look and refused to admit that her feet were already swollen uncomfortably in the heat. She was wondering if she would even make it as far as the ute.

This was even worse than she had imagined! She had had no idea how *far* everything was in Australia. When Guy had picked her up that afternoon, she had been ready, cool and polite, and affronted when he demanded rudely what she thought she was wearing.

'Travelling clothes.' She had glanced down at herself, wondering what all the fuss was about. It was only when she tried to clamber up on to the wing of the little plane that the disadvantage of narrow skirt and high heels had dawned. 'You might have told me we were flying,' she complained. 'I thought we'd be going by car.'

'We're going a bit further than the suburbs,' Guy had said. 'I assumed you'd realise that we'd fly when I said we'd be back at Willagong tonight. How long do you think it would take us to drive?'

Olivia had snapped her fingers, as if remembering. 'Damn! I left my crystal ball back at the hotel!' she'd said sarcastically.

Guy had eyed her with dislike. 'It's going to take us over two hours to fly,' he'd said. 'I'll let you work out how long that would be in a car. Now hurry up and get in!'

The flight had seemed interminable. From the air, the country had looked as dry and red and empty as sandpaper under the aching blue bowl of the sky. The horizon stretched into infinity in every direction. Olivia's only consolation was that they weren't in fact in a car. She hated to think what it would be like to drive through.

It was a relief to be on the ground again. Sitting cooped up next to Guy for so long had made her twitchy. She had been uncomfortably aware of him, her eyes straying almost against their will to his hands, strong and capable on the joystick, and his profile, unyielding against the sky. Olivia would jerk her head away as soon as she realised she was staring and look straight ahead at the blur of the propeller instead, but before long her gaze would slide back to Guy once more. If she looked at his mouth too long she would begin to feel a curl of warmth, hastily suppressed. His lips looked firm, inflexible even; there was just something suggestive about them that left her feeling . . . well, restless.

'By the way,' he said, hauling her suitcases into the open back of the ute, 'I haven't told David you're his guardian. As far as he's concerned, you're just a friend who's coming to visit.'

'How does he know I'm coming?' Olivia asked suspiciously.

He opened the van door with what she was sure was mock courtesy. 'Let's say I anticipated that you'd want to come out and see him straight away.'

'And you said *I* pushed people around!' Olivia said crossly, disliking the idea that she had done exactly what he wanted. She brushed fastidiously at the dust lying thickly on the bench seat before lowering herself with care on to the clean patch. It looked like the end of her cream skirt! 'Don't worry, I won't spring anything on him, but I warn you that I'm not likely to forget that I'm his guardian.'

He shrugged as he started the engine. 'I'm surprised you're so determined to have David. From what I've heard of you, I'd have thought you'd have been glad of any excuse to get rid of him so that you could concentrate on your career and your social life.'

'I might say the same of you,' Olivia said frostily. 'It's odd for a bachelor to want to give up his freedom for a child.'

Guy didn't answer immediately. 'I like David,' he said eventually. 'And Pete was my friend as well as my cousin. He used to love the outback; I know he always felt bad that his job meant that David had to grow up in a town.'

I like David. Olivia was silent, thinking about the boy she was responsible for. Would *she* like him? She had been so taken up with doing what Diane would have wanted that she hadn't really thought about what David was like. She had never had much to do with children. What if she didn't like him? What if he didn't like *her*?

'See that line of trees over there?' Guy broke into her thoughts. 'That's Willagong Creek.' His voice for once was warm with enthusiasm, and Olivia eyed him curiously. What was there to love in this sunburnt country?

True, it wasn't quite as empty as it had appeared from the air, with the slender gums, rocky outcrops and, here and there, bizarrely-shaped termite mounds rising out of the red ground, but to Olivia, city girl through and through, the sense of space and vast silence was strangely intimidating.

She was no more impressed by her first sight of the homestead, a long, low building set among the trees, its corrugated iron roof flashing in the fierce outback light and dipping low to shelter the house with a deep, dim veranda. A cluster of dilapidated wooden buildings stood a little distance away across a dusty yard, presided over by a tall wind tower, its arms quite still in the heavy heat.

'There's David.' Guy's voice brought Olivia's attention back to the house. A small boy was sitting on the veranda steps.

Olivia took a long breath, stupidly nervous now. She would hardly have recognised him. The chubby five-year-old had grown into a thin, gangly child with stuck-out ears and a rather serious face. But his eyes were Diane's and his smile, as he saw Guy, was Diane's too. Olivia swallowed, her heart twisting with the memory of her friend.

Glancing over at Guy, in an unconscious appeal for support, she stopped dead, the breath driven from her lungs as if by a kick in the stomach. For he was not looking at her. He was looking at David, and he was smiling. The brown man, the ordinary man, had snapped into colour. His teeth were very white and his smile was warm, deepening the creases in his cheeks and at the edges of his eyes.

Thrown off balance by her unexpectedly physical reaction, Olivia looked away. It was only a smile. She began to breathe again, very carefully. In, out. In, out. Easy.

'This is Olivia. She was a great friend of your mother's.' Guy had his hand on David's shoulder as he turned him to face her. He wasn't smiling now.

Olivia pulled herself together. 'Hello, David,' she said gently. 'You probably don't remember me.'

David shook his head, too young for diplomacy. 'No.'

'Well, perhaps we'll be able to get to know each other again.' Olivia smiled awkwardly.

David didn't seem to think this required a reply. There was a pause. Olivia bit her lip. Somehow she had imagined that she and David would rush into each other's arms for comfort, but there was an air of tension about the little boy that warned her against any affectionate demonstration.

Instinctively, she glanced at Guy again, and this time he responded. 'Olivia's going to stay a few days,' he said. 'Why don't you find her a bedroom, David, and show her the homestead, while I go and talk to the boys? There are sheets in the cupboard in my bedroom. I'll bring the cases in later.' With a nod, he reached into the cab of the ute for his hat, settled it on his head and strolled off, leaving Olivia and David looking after him rather uncertainly.

Olivia found her voice first. She was surprised that Guy had left her alone with David so easily. She had almost expected him to try and make things difficult for her. She glanced down at David. 'Well—er—lead on, David!'

She followed him up the steps and into the dark cool of the house, dismayed by peeling paint and evidence of neglect. Once inside, she stared around her, appalled. 'Have you been *living* here?' she demanded. It looked as if it had not been cleaned for at least twenty years. Cobwebs shrouded the ceiling and a thick red blanket of dust lay eerily over everything. The only sign of life was the trail of footprints connecting the bathroom, two bedrooms and the veranda. Guy and David were obviously creatures of routine.

David looked about him in surprise, wondering why she seemed so horrified. 'Guy and me sleep here at night,' he told her, 'but we have all our meals in the cookhouse with the ringers.'

'Ringers?' she queried.

'They're the stockmen. There's Corky and Ben and Darren and Joe. Ben takes me out roo shooting sometimes.'

'What?' Olivia exclaimed in horror. 'You mean you shoot *kangaroos*? How could you?'

'Roos are a pest,' he informed her kindly.

'I see.' Olivia's lips tightened. These were no conditions to bring up a child. Not only was David

living in filth, but he was being taken out and shown
how to kill innocent animals with a gun! The sooner
she got him out of here the better!

'What do you do when you're not sleeping and
eating?' she asked.

'I go riding with Guy sometimes. Sometimes I
go down to the creek.'

'Don't you ever . . . I don't know . . . sit and read?
Watch television?'

David looked blank. 'There isn't a television.' He
scratched his nose, trying to think of something else
they did. 'We sit on the veranda and have a beer
every evening before supper.'

'Guy never gives you *beer*!' Olivia's voice rose
slightly.

'Sometimes he lets me have a bit,' David amended
reluctantly. 'Mostly I have lemonade.'

Relieved, Olivia opened a door into a large,
bright bedroom. One of the shutters was falling off
and it was shrouded in dust like everywhere else,
but the bed looked solid enough. 'I'll have this as
my bedroom, shall I?' She looked down at him
wryly. 'I don't suppose you know where there's a
brush?'

'Yes, I do.' David heaved a big sigh. 'Guy makes
me clean my room out every day.'

Olivia lifted an eyebrow in surprise. Cleaning
didn't seem to be a priority round here. 'I'm glad
to hear it,' she said in a dry voice.

## CHAPTER TWO

DAVID found her the broom and even volunteered to sweep the floor for her. Olivia was touched, watching him manfully wield the long broom, and tactfully didn't point out all the places he had missed. She was delighted that, after his initial air of reserve, he seemed to have opened up as he chattered about the ringers and riding and exactly how many different species of insect there were to be found down in the creek.

'What about your lessons?' she asked, then cursed herself as a shadow crossed his face.

He bent his head over the broom. 'I used to go to school in Brisbane, but I don't go any more.'

'Shall we go and find some sheets?' she said gently, dropping a hand on to his shoulder. Now was not the time to bring back painful memories of his parents' death.

Guy's room was further down the corridor. Olivia was curiously shy of entering, but she was anxious to divert David. Hesitating on the threshold, she looked about her, as David began foraging in the cupboard. This room at least was scrupulously clean. It was typical of the man, she thought, plain and uncompromising. No pictures, no decoration, no clues to his personality.

Her eyes slid to the heavy iron bed and then away. She didn't want to think about how Guy would look in bed.

Restlessly, she walked over to the window. The afternoon was fading rapidly, the harsh light softening to a glow. In the distance she could see Guy standing by the stockyards, talking to two men. They were all dressed identically, in jeans and shirts and hats, but even at this distance Guy's aura of quiet, coiled strength was unmistakable.

As she watched, he nodded, said something to the two men and turned to walk with that peculiarly deliberate pace towards the homestead. Hastily she stepped back from the window. She didn't want him to think she'd been staring at him.

'I've got the sheets.' David was looking at her with an odd expression. 'What were you staring at?'

'Oh—er—just the trees.' Olivia took the sheets from him. 'Thank you for your help, David. Just show me where the shower is and I'll look after myself.'

The screen door creaked as she pushed it open and stepped out on to the veranda. Guy was leaning on the rail, looking out at a dramatic red sunset, a can of beer in his hand. He straightened and turned as he heard her, then put the can very carefully on to the rail. For no reason Olivia felt her blood begin to pound slowly, insistently, through her veins.

Wrapping her arms about her, she advanced almost nervously. Her cases had appeared in her room while she was showering, so that she had been able to change into a deceptively simple black T-shirt dress, cinched at the waist with a wide leather belt. Her hair, newly washed, hung shiny and silky to her jaw.

There was a momentary silence as Guy's eyes rested on her, then flickered away. 'Find everything you needed?' he asked.

'Yes, thank you.' Olivia wandered over to the rail to stand a little way away from him. 'I thought I'd find you here. I gather you don't use the rest of the house.'

'Not at the moment. It's not in a fit state for much.' He picked up his can again. 'It's a long time since there's been a woman at Willagong Creek.'

'You don't need a woman, you need a dustpan and brush!' Olivia pointed out sharply.

'And time,' Guy said. 'I only bought this property last year.'

'Oh? I had the impression you were born and bred in the outback.'

'I was. My family have got a place over near Cloncurry. It's a good property—one of the best—but I wanted to make a go on my own.'

'Didn't you ever want to do anything else?' Olivia asked, interested despite herself.

'Like what? Sitting in an office?'

'There are other options,' she pointed out.

Guy leant on the rail once more and stared out to where the gums cut off the distant horizon. 'I know. I did an engineering degree, and worked in South Australia for a couple of years, but my heart wasn't in it. The land pulls you back. It's hard to explain. It's just part of you.'

'But don't you ever get bored?' Olivia gestured at the silent view. 'Don't you ever want to go somewhere new, see something other than dust and gums?'

He glanced at her, a tug of amusement, or maybe contempt, at the corner of his mouth. 'Is that all you see? Dust and gums?' He shook his head. 'I go to Europe and America occasionally to buy bulls or meet the buyers, but I'd be just as happy to stay here.

'Willagong is a fine property,' he added slowly, almost as if he wanted her to understand. 'It got swallowed up by some company twenty years ago, and no one's lived here since. They sold it off as a single lot last year when the company broke up the property again. It's good land, but it hasn't been looked after. It would have been a lot easier to have stayed on the family property, but there's nothing like knowing it's your own land. My father taught me how to run a property, but he inherited his from his father. I've got a chance here to start from scratch, to make my own mistakes. I'm bringing the land back to life—slowly.' He stopped abruptly, as if realising how much he had revealed about himself. 'I've got a lot to do before I worry about a bit of dusting,' he finished, with a conscious effort to lighten the mood.

'A bit of dusting!' Olivia teased, following his lead. 'You've got half the Simpson Desert in there!'

He shrugged. 'It's not that bad.' He glanced down at the can in his hand. 'Want a beer?'

'Actually, I'd love a——' There wasn't going to be anything else, was there? 'Beer would be fine,' she said resignedly.

She lowered herself into one of the sagging wicker chairs. Something in her had stirred in response to Guy's evident feeling for his property. She understood the need to make it on your own, to throw yourself body and soul into making your job a success. Perhaps Guy was not so different.

The memory of his smile was still uncomfortably vivid. Who else apart from David was privileged to be smiled at like that? He had family, presumably he had friends, girlfriends. Did he smile at them? Olivia's eyes narrowed at the thought of Guy's girlfriends. What kind of girl did he like? Whatever, it obviously wasn't her kind! She had never met a man who was so unresponsive to her looks.

'Here.' Guy reappeared and handed her a can. It was so cold that she was glad of the polystyrene holder to protect her hands.

'Thank you,' she murmured, deciding against asking for a glass. Pulling the tab awkwardly, she look a sip. It was deliciously cold and wet in her dry throat. She hadn't realised quite how thirsty she was.

'How did you get on with David?' Guy asked, settling himself in the chair beside her. It creaked alarmingly.

'Quite well, I think.' Olivia looked down at the can she held. 'He's a nice boy.'

'Yes, he is. Diane and Pete brought him up well.'

Another silence fell. It was very quiet and still as the fiery glow of sunset deepened and darkened. Somewhere in the background, a generator throbbed and, unknown and unseen, insects whirred shrilly beneath the gums.

Guy sat forward in his chair, arms resting on his knees as he turned the beer can thoughtfully between his hands. Olivia felt herself slowly relax. Less than a week ago, she thought, she'd have been fighting her way through the London traffic, pushing on to the Tube, jostling with the other commuters, in a rush to get home and then out to the bright lights again. It all seemed so unreal. Real was now: the red sky and the silver gleam of the gums through the dusk and the man sitting so still and thoughtful beside her.

Suddenly the gums erupted in a blur of white wings as a flock of cockatoos took off together in response to some unheard signal. Startled out of her reverie, Olivia glanced sideways at Guy, to find him watching her with an unreadable expression in his deep eyes.

'It's not such a bad place, is it?' he said quietly.

Olivia dragged her eyes away and took a hasty sip of her beer. 'Most places look nice at sunset,' she said, hoping her voice sounded steadier than she felt. 'I'm still far from convinced that this is the right place for David to be. The house is awful; all he seems to do is roam around outside. His main entertainment seems to be shooting kangaroos with somebody called Ben.'

'I'm afraid shooting roos is a fact of life out here. They eat the grass that we need for our stock.'

'But they're such lovely creatures! It's terrible to think of a boy being taught to destroy them!'

'You need to be more than pretty to survive in the outback, Olivia.' Guy's eyes rested on her significantly and she tilted her chin at him. 'David isn't learning to enjoy killing. He's being taught how to do what's necessary, as painlessly as possible. In any case,' he went on, 'they don't shoot that many. Mostly it's just an excuse for them to wander off. Ben's good with David. He tells him the things he wants to know, and he learns a lot more that way than he would sitting in front of a television, which is no doubt what he'd be doing in the evenings in London.'

'Not necessarily.' Olivia stubbornly refused to meet his eyes. What *would* she do with David in the evenings? 'Anyway, television can be very educational.'

At that moment David came running through the rapidly deepening gloom, arms and legs sticking out in different directions. 'Corky says supper's in fifteen minutes.' He puffed up the steps. 'Can I have some beer tonight, Guy?'

'No,' said Olivia firmly, before Guy had a chance to reply.

David stuck out his lower lip and looked pleadingly at Guy, obviously unwilling to accept Olivia's authority.

'You heard what the lady said,' Guy said surprisingly, softening his siding with the opposition

with another heart-shaking smile. He jerked his
head towards the kitchen, whose sole function was
to house the fridge full of cold drinks. 'Go and
find yourself a lemonade.'

'A sip every now and then doesn't do him any
harm,' he said to Olivia as David scuffed his way
along the veranda.

'He's far too young to be even thinking about
beer,' Olivia said crossly, more to disguise her
alarming reaction to his smile than from any real
conviction. She had a peculiar sensation inside, as
if something was squeezing tightly. To make things
worse, the smile was still lurking about his mouth.
Not the smile he had given David, but the tantalising, elusive remains, as if he found her secretly
amusing.

As he turned his head away, she let her breath
out slowly. What was the matter with her? She
didn't normally go all weak at the knees just because a man smiled.

Jet lag, she told herself firmly.

Guy raised his can again. Olivia watched his
hands—they were neat, long, almost slender, with
quick, sure fingers.

She jerked her eyes away. She wished she could
think of something to say, but her mind wouldn't
function beyond an awareness of hands and mouth.
She drank her beer desperately. Why couldn't Guy
say something? He seemed quite unbothered by the
silence.

Fortunately David came skidding back along the
veranda then and she was able to concentrate on

him, resolutely ignoring Guy, drinking in unperturbed silence beside her.

They walked over to the cookhouse through the
darkness which had dropped with disconcerting
speed. The ringers all stood up as Olivia came in,
and looked down at their feet.

Olivia, at ease in the most intimidating of cocktail
parties, felt ridiculously awkward. 'Hello,' she said
brightly, then winced at the sound of her own voice.
Did she always sound that English?

They mumbled, 'Evening,' and shook the hand
she held out hesitantly to each in turn as David per-
formed the introductions. Corky, a dour, wiry little
man, was the eldest. Ben—the kangaroo killer,
Olivia remembered acidly—was rather good-
looking, and probably only a couple of years
younger than Guy. Darren and Joe, lanky boys of
about twenty, eyed each other uneasily, managing
successfully to make Olivia feel like some gaudy,
alien creature. How long was it since they'd seen a
woman? she wondered waspishly, unaware of the
effect of her vivid beauty and the indefinable air
of glamour that clung to her in those plain
surroundings.

The cookhouse was rectangular, with painted
wooden walls a faded, yellowish shade of white in
the light of a single, naked light bulb. At the far
end of the room stood a vast, old-fashioned stove,
and an array of wooden cupboards. There was a
table in the middle of the cooking area, piled high
with huge, blackened pots, a deep double sink and
three heavy fridges lined up against the walls like

sentinels. Olivia thought of her hygienic, stream-lined kitchen in London and sighed.

There was some awkward shuffling and scraping of chairs as they took their places at the long wooden table. Corky, who appeared to be the cook, deposited a plate piled high with boiled potatoes, overcooked cabbage and dry grey meat in front of her.

'This looks delicious—er—Corky,' she tried valiantly. Was that really his name? She averted her eyes from his grimy hands. 'What else do you cook apart from roast...um...' what was it? beef? mutton? '...apart from roast?'

'I don't cook nothing else,' Corky answered, taciturn. 'We always have roast.'

'What, every night?'

He merely grunted. Appalled, Olivia looked down at the gravy congealing on her plate and suppressed a shudder. 'What about lunch?'

'Cold meat,' volunteered Darren, and immediately flushed to the roots of his carroty hair.

'And steak for breakfast,' Joe added.

'So, how many of you are vegetarian?' Olivia's teasing glance encountered blank looks. Only Guy's level eyes met hers with understanding and that unsettling trace of amusement.

She relapsed into silence as he changed the conversation to the work to be done the next day. Their incomprehensible stockmen's jargon meant nothing to her, and she was able to study Guy covertly while they talked. She was struck again by the tough, brown look these men shared, but where Corky's face was seamed and Joe's round, Ben's hair curly and Darren's unruly, there was nothing to soften the austere lines of Guy's features. Firm nose, firm chin, firm mouth. He had a sparse, uncluttered look about him, she thought, her eyes drifting down the column of his throat to powerful shoulders. His blue cotton shirt was open at the neck and there was just a glimpse of strong brown chest.

Aware that her imagination was beginning to wander dangerously, Olivia bent her head to her plate once more. She ploughed her way through the meal and wondered instead about how soon she would be able to break the news to David that they were leaving. There was no way she was going to stay in this place a minute longer than she had to!

Olivia spent the next morning wandering rather aimlessly around the homestead. Guy and the ringers had ridden off long before she was awake, David informed her, when he met her picking her way in high heels down the rough track to the stockyards.

'Oh.' She hesitated. Guy might at least have waited around until she was up! She had had to find her own breakfast in that disgusting kitchen, and it looked as if she was going to have to amuse herself somehow. 'Where are you off to?' she asked David.

'I'm going for a ride. I've got my own horse,' he said proudly. 'Do you want to see him?'

'All right.' Suspecting that this was something of an honour, Olivia turned and followed him to the paddock. She was rather wary of horses. They had a nasty habit of rolling their eyes at you, and her one attempt to learn how to ride had left her determined never to go near a horse again. She stayed firmly behind the wooden rails as David called to a solid-looking bay pony and slipped on its bridle.

Olivia was impressed, but kept at a safe distance when David led the pony over proudly. 'What's his name?' she asked.

'Topper. Guy gave him to me for my very own.' David's face was alight as he stroked the animal's glossy neck.

It looked an awfully big horse to Olivia. 'Are you allowed to go riding by yourself?' she asked nervously.

'Course I am!' He threw her a scornful glance. 'Guy says I'm a good rider. When I'm older he says I can go on musters and ride in the rodeo.' No prizes for guessing who David's hero was!

She watched him saddle the pony with surprising ease. 'Are you Guy's new girlfriend?' he asked unexpectedly as he tightened the girth.

*New* girlfriend? Olivia's long eyes glittered suddenly green. Who was the *old* girlfriend? 'Not exactly,' she said carefully. 'Why do you ask?'

David shrugged. 'Ben asked me,' he said, patently not much interested.

'Oh.' She hesitated. She shouldn't really pump a child for information, but there wasn't anyone else to ask. 'Does Guy already have a girlfriend, then?' she asked casually.

'I expect so.' David was preoccupied with checking the saddle and evidently didn't feel the matter was worthy of much consideration.

Olivia regarded him with frustration. 'Does he ever bring her here?' she persevered.

'Who?'

'His girlfriend.' Her patience was beginning to fray.

David scratched his head. 'I don't know.'

Hardly a mine of information! 'Oh, well, it doesn't matter,' said Olivia, resolving to talk to Ben instead. 'Have a nice ride.'

She walked slowly back to the house. The girlfriend obviously wasn't a permanent enough feature to register with David... She caught herself up guiltily. Why was she so interested in Guy's girlfriend anyway? Then she reassured herself hastily. Any prospect of Guy's marrying would affect David, though, wouldn't it?

*If* she left David here.

Olivia's face was thoughtful as she climbed the steps and wandered from silent room to silent room. She *couldn't* leave him somewhere like this... and yet he seemed so much happier than she had expected. Did she have the right to take him away from all that was familiar?

Arguments for and against leaving David with Guy circled uselessly, until, in a fit of restlessness, she seized the broom from the kitchen and began to brush the years of dust from the living area just inside the front door. She might as well do something useful while she was doing her thinking!

The mindless task was curiously soothing. Before she came out to Willagong Creek, her mind had been a ferment of plans: what to do about David's schooling, when to book a flight back to London, keeping in touch with the contacts she mustn't lose if she was going to make a success of a freelance touring company... She hadn't thought about any of it since she arrived, she realised with an obscure lack of surprise.

Really, it wasn't such a bad room, now she came to look at it. An air of quiet and peace pervaded the house, and with the worst of the dust brushed away, she could almost imagine how it might have been before it had been abandoned. Her eyes fell on an old clock on the mantelpiece and she wound it up, with the fanciful notion that she might wind the house into life again as easily.

Closing her eyes, she stood in the middle of the room and turned slowly as the clock ticked into the silence. She could see it all quite clearly. The walls would be cleaned and repainted, the wooden floors polished and gleaming. Outside, the neglected garden might be cajoled back into life. Her imagination drifted. Guy would be coming up the veranda steps, smiling. Funny, she could visualise him with startling clarity, as if every line on his face was familiar to her and——

'Olivia?'

Startled, Olivia's eyes, soft and blue with dreaming, flew open. Guy was propped in the doorway, almost blocking out the rectangle of harsh sunlight, one long leg casually crossed in front of the other, hands thrust into the pockets of his jeans.

He wore his stockman's hat as if it were part of him, she thought inconsequentially, unsettled by the way her heart had jolted at the sight of him.

'Funny place to fall asleep,' he observed as he took off his hat and advanced into the room, brushing the dust off the brim.

'I wasn't asleep. I was . . . thinking.'

'What about?'

*You.* 'Oh . . . nothing.' Olivia was suddenly awkward and tongue-tied, acutely aware of his lean brown strength. She felt embarrassed, as if his perceptive eyes had seen exactly what she had been dreaming about.

Guy raised an eyebrow at her evasive answer, but didn't comment. 'I saw David disappearing off. I thought you'd want him to stay with you.'

'I don't want to tie him down,' she said defensively.

'Don't you? That's what you'll do if you take him to a town.'

She bit her lip, turned away from him. Better not to rise to the bait. 'He certainly seems very keen on his horse,' she said in a non-committal voice.

'He's a cracking little rider,' Guy agreed. She could feel his eyes on her. 'You're good with him.'

It was so unexpected that she swung back in astonishment. 'Me?'

'I noticed last night. You talked to him as if he was a person, not a baby. You didn't try to smother him with affection either. David wouldn't like that.'

Olivia felt absurdly pleased by the laconic praise. She had always thought of herself as being hopeless with children.

Guy laid his hat on the heavy sideboard. 'Have you thought any more about what you're going to do about David?'

'I haven't been thinking about anything else,' Olivia said wryly, and not quite truthfully. She had wasted an awful lot of time thinking about Guy himself.

'Come to any conclusions?'

'Not yet.' She picked up the broom and began sweeping again. She wasn't about to be bamboozled into making any hurried decisions. 'Only that you could do with a new cook!'

A gleam of amusement sprang to Guy's eyes. 'Corky's better on a horse than in the kitchen— but he cooks better than the other boys, believe me. When I get around to finding a housekeeper, she can take over. Corky's too valuable outside to have him tied to the kitchen.'

His eyes rested on Olivia, typically elegant in a blue and white sprigged dress, heels and chunky earrings. It looked all wrong with the broom. A shaft of sunlight through the doorway lit the gold in her hair and illuminated a thousand dancing motes of dust around her. 'You shouldn't be cleaning dressed like that,' he said, almost roughly.

Olivia looked down at herself, as if noticing her dress for the first time. It was looking rather grubby. She was usually the first person to recoil at the thought of getting dirty, but now she merely shrugged. 'Oh, well... the room looks better, though, doesn't it?'

Guy glanced around, but his gaze returned to Olivia. 'Yes,' he agreed, 'I suppose it does.'

Across the room, their eyes met, and for Olivia it was as if the ticking clock and the slowly drifting dust had stopped with the beat of her heart. Suspended in time, unable to breathe, she could only stare back at Guy. She couldn't read the expression on his face. All she knew was that the latent hostility had suddenly gone, and that his eyes held her in thrall.

And then the sound of eager footsteps broke the spell. The clock resumed its ticking, the dust continued its languid descent, her heart hammered back into life. She found she was clutching the broom as if for support, and very gradually loosened her grip. What on earth was the matter with her? The indifferent look had dropped back over Guy's face so utterly that she wondered if she had been imagining things.

'Look what I've found!' David burst through the screen door, his hands cupped in front of him.

'What is it?' Guy asked, peering down as David eased his hands apart just enough for him to see. He nodded, impressed. 'Take a look at this, Olivia.'

How could he sound so normal? Hadn't he felt anything just now? Still taken up with that odd little interlude, she leant down incuriously to inspect David's prize.

In his hands he held the most enormous spider she had ever seen.

This time she thought her heart really was going to stop. She felt the hairs at the back of her neck rise in cold horror as the blood drained from her face and the scream clogged in her throat. She had always had a phobia about spiders, and to have this one, evil and grotesque, thrust under her nose was more than she could bear!

'Take it out!' she croaked, backing away, and then, when David only looked surprised and then aggrieved, her voice rose in shrill panic. 'Take it out! Take it out! Take it *out*!'

'I think she wants you to take it out,' Guy said to David, dry amusement in his voice.

The look they had exchanged was forgotten. Olivia hated him, hated his condescending amusement, hated David's long-suffering sigh as he trudged outside. Her voice shook as she wrapped her arms about her protectively and glared at Guy. 'It's not funny!' she snapped.

'Take it easy, Olivia. It's only a spider.'

'Only!' She pressed the back of her hand to her mouth to try and stop it shaking. 'It was horrible! And you—you just encouraged him! Did you do it deliberately? Did you think it would be a good trick to frighten me? Was it part of some plan to make me go away?' She was teetering on the edge of hysteria.

'Don't be silly!' Guy took her by the shoulders and shook her sharply. His hands were hard against the bare skin of her arms and she felt his strength flow through her. 'David brought the spider because he thought you'd be as interested as he is in insects. He didn't mean to frighten you. He just wanted to show it off.' Almost absently, he rubbed his thumbs against the soft skin of her upper arms, holding her firmly, as he might quieten a frightened horse. His touch was curiously reassuring.

'How could he pick it up?' Olivia shuddered. She pulled away from Guy's grip. The hysteria had subsided, but illogical resentment bubbled at how easily he had calmed her with touch rather than words. 'How can you let him go around picking up things like that? There are all sorts of poisonous creatures out there! What if something bit him? He might be killed!'

'David knows what's poisonous and what isn't,' Guy said steadily. 'There's no point in being over-protective. Some boys like trains, some boys like soldiers, David likes insects. That's just the way he is, and you're going to have to accept that, because he's going to be the same wherever he is. If you can't deal with the fact that he's a small boy, you shouldn't be dealing with him at all.' He retrieved his hat from the sideboard and settled it on his head. 'I'll leave you to think about it.' With a last look at her rigid countenance, he walked out, leaving her standing alone in the middle of the room.

Olivia couldn't sleep. Pushing back the wooden shutters, she leant on the windowsill and stared out at the night. It was utterly quiet, the blackness lit only by the light of the massy stars of the southern hemisphere.

'Oh, Diane, what should I do?' she murmured. She desperately wanted to do what was best for David, both for his sake and for Diane's. She had been so sure of what to do before Guy Richardson had interfered, she thought bitterly. Now she just didn't know.

She thought about her flat in London. It had been a new conversion, conveniently central, practical, tastefully decorated. She liked being at the top of the house, liked having no garden to look after. But how would David cope somewhere like that? There would be nowhere for him to play, nowhere to run, no horrible insects to collect.

She could move, of course... 'Where?' she asked herself honestly. She would never be able to afford a big house with a garden. She could certainly never give David a horse to ride or a creek to play in. She had to work to support herself—and David now—and her job had to be based in London. Coming to Australia had been a way to run away from Tim and the thought of all those wasted years for a while, but she couldn't stay. She knew from Diane that Australian immigration rules were very strict, and she would never get the right kind of visa at her age, even if she had wanted to stay. She would have to go back to face Tim and his new wife and sympathetic friends eventually.

But how would David fit in with her career and her smart, sophisticated friends? Guy's comments about her social life were unfair, but it would still be hard for her to stay in with a little boy knowing that friends were out at parties or concerts or restaurants.

Up until now she had led such a selfish existence, she realised. Her parents had died when she was not much older than David—she knew a little of what he felt—and since then she'd really only ever had herself to consider.

Now she had to think about David.

It was scary to feel so responsible. Olivia swallowed. Her first thoughts had been about herself, hadn't they? How much she was going to miss Diane. How her life was going to have to change because of David. She hadn't realised then that Diane had trusted her to do what was best for her son.

David was happier here than he would be with her in London, she acknowledged reluctantly. And Guy was right, she had no idea how to cope with a small boy. He would be far better off here, in spite of the isolation, the lack of schools and hospitals and playgrounds.

Tomorrow she would go to Guy and tell him that she would leave David with him after all.

## CHAPTER THREE

HER decision made, Olivia relaxed slightly, only to tense again as the muffled sound of a child's crying broke the stillness of the night.

*David.* She hesitated. Would he want her to see him crying? Weren't little boys proud about that kind of thing?

But she couldn't just stand here and listen to a child sobbing! Shrugging herself into the dark blue silk kimono she had bought on her last trip to Japan, she slipped out of her room and down to David's closed door. She knocked softly.

'David?'

He was lying face down on the bed, thin shoulders heaving, racked by sobs. Olivia's heart cracked. He was only small.

'David,' she said again, sitting down on the bed and pulling him gently on to her lap.

He resisted at first. 'I want Mum!' he cried desperately, struggling against unfamiliar arms.

'I know.' Olivia held him tightly. 'I know you do, David,' she whispered, and he gave in abruptly and buried himself against her. Heavy and sodden with grief, he cried for his mother and for his father and for all the love and security that had been wiped out by a drunken driver on the Pacific Highway.

The tears slid unheeded down Olivia's face as she rocked him instinctively, murmuring soothing, meaningless words of comfort. Who would have thought that the rather cocky little boy who had showed off his pony would have had all this bottled up inside him?

'Mum had a dress just like the one you wore tonight,' David told her at last, between shuddering breaths. 'It was her best dress. She wore it to the school barbecue...'

'I'm sorry, David. I didn't know.'

'It's just... I was thinking about her... Mostly I try not to...'

Olivia sat on, holding him, letting him talk in halting, jerky sentences, resting her cheek on the sweet-smelling, childish head where the tousled hair grew in obstinately different directions. Once she glanced up to see Guy in the doorway, watching her with a questioning look, but she laid a finger against her lips and he nodded, leaving her alone with David once more.

At last he began to drift asleep. Olivia smoothed out his sheets as best she could and laid him down tenderly. 'I'm sorry about the spider. Mum didn't like spiders either,' he mumbled, only just awake, and then, 'You're not going to go away just yet, are you?'

Olivia looked down at him, an odd expression on her face. 'No, David,' she said, but so quietly that he probably didn't hear as he slipped into sleep, 'I won't go away.'

\*     \*     \*

From the veranda, she watched Guy and David ride past along the trail towards the paddock. Guy's horse towered over David's pony. He sat easily in the saddle, head bent down to the boy chattering beside him.

David appeared to be none the worse for his outburst last night. Olivia wondered if he even remembered. She certainly wished she felt that fresh and bright. She had fallen into an uneasy sleep long after she had left David's room, and now her head ached and her body buzzed with exhaustion.

Resting her head back against the battered wicker with a sigh, she forced herself to think about the arguments once more. David would be happiest staying at Willagong Creek, she had decided that. But last night had shown her that he was much more vulnerable than he had appeared. It was different now. Holding the small, unhappy child last night had awoken in her a fierce protectiveness that she had not known she possessed. She couldn't just walk away from Diane's son, she couldn't leave David behind knowing that he might need her, however rarely. He might have a horse and a creek, but he was only eight. He needed a mother too.

He would hate living in London. And she had promised that she would stay.

Olivia glanced around her, at the dusty wooden floor, at the sagging shutter and the peeling paint. Outside the glare bounced off every surface and the corrugated-iron roof of the cookhouse flashed in the unrelenting sun. A fly settled on her hand and she brushed it away irritably.

She would hate living here.

The idea that had come to her in the early hours of the morning had been so startling that at first she had dismissed it out of hand, but she was still thinking about it now in broad daylight. It might work...if only she could pluck up the courage...

Olivia stood up suddenly, her mind made up. She could see Guy in the distance, walking with that deliberate gait of his towards the sheds.

The glare hit her as she ran lightly down the steps and waved to him. 'Guy!'

He stopped, turned to watch her shade her eyes with one hand and beckon to him again. Her hair glittered like gilt in the sunlight.

He never hurried, Olivia thought with a flash of irritation, hastily suppressed. This wasn't the time to get snappy with him. By the time he reached her, she had a bright smile on her face, and his eyes narrowed suspiciously.

'What is it?' he demanded.

It wasn't a promising beginning. With his cool, watchful eyes on her face, Olivia's confidence in her sudden bright idea began to falter. Come on, she chided herself. You're Olivia Bridewell, famed for her poise in difficult situations!

'Er—could I talk to you for a minute?'

'Can't it wait till later?' He obviously wasn't going to be helpful.

'I'd rather talk to you now.' Olivia had to screw up her eyes against the glare. 'Look, it's so bright out here. Can't we sit on the veranda? It won't take long.'

Guy shrugged, but followed her back to the welcome shade. The chair creaked as he sat down next to her. 'I suppose you're going to tell me that you're going to take David away?' he said flatly.

She glanced at him in surprise. 'What makes you say that?'

'I saw you with him last night, remember?' He hesitated, as if remembering the scene: the sobbing child clutching for comfort, being cradled against softness and blue silk, Olivia's bright hair, tousled for once, falling forward as she rested her cheek on his head, her eyes shadowed. 'I imagined you were going to tell me he needs a mother.'

'Doesn't he?'

There was a pause. 'Perhaps.' Guy looked out at the dusty yard shimmering in the heat. 'But I think he needs this kind of life more. I promise I'll get a good woman in to look after him.'

'That's what I wanted to talk to you about, actually.' Olivia steeled herself as he turned his head in surprise. 'You haven't appointed anyone yet, have you?'

'No,' he said, obviously wondering where this was leading.

'Why not let me be your housekeeper?'

'*You?*' He stared at her incredulously. 'A housekeeper?'

Olivia licked her lips nervously. 'Why not?'

He looked at her. She had made an effort to look more practical and was wearing narrow stone-coloured trousers and a white sleeveless top, but the effect was somehow only to make her look more sophisticated. Leaning forward, he took one of her hands and inspected it. 'Look at this hand,' he said. Olivia followed his gaze down to where it lay, soft, slim, perfectly manicured in his hold, and wondered how it was possible to feel so aware of every single millimetre of his skin touching hers. 'This hasn't done much rough work, has it?' He gave her back her hand as if it were a parcel. 'I need someone who's not afraid of getting her hands dirty.'

Olivia's mouth was set in a determined line. 'I can work,' she said stubbornly. 'I can clean and cook as well as the next person—if not better.' She lifted her chin proudly. 'I've got a cordon bleu certificate.'

'Fancy cooking's not much use out here,' Guy pointed out, patently unimpressed.

'I'm sure with a little practice I could learn to cook as badly as Corky, if that's what you want!' she snapped before she could help herself.

His eyes narrowed. 'Are you serious about this?'

'Yes, I am.' Olivia stood up restlessly and went to stand by the veranda rail, not looking at Guy. 'I've thought and I've thought, and it makes sense. You're right, David would hate London. I think he should grow up here, but he's just a little boy. He needs someone to look after him properly, and I want it to be me.' She turned back to face him. 'That means me staying here as well. You need a housekeeper anyway...it seems like the obvious solution.'

Guy was sitting forward, staring down at his hands clasped loosely between his knees. He lifted his head as she finished to look at her, his eyes dark and intent. 'And what about your oh, so important career?'

She met his gaze squarely. 'I'd resigned my job so I could set up as a freelance. I can still do that. It'll just mean waiting a little while.' She hesitated. It was hard explaining just how much her career meant to her. She loved the people and the planning and the travel. More importantly, it was something she had achieved for herself. It wasn't going to be easy without the stimulation of colleagues or the adrenalin-pumping approach of deadlines, but she didn't think Guy would understand that. 'David won't need me forever,' was all she said.

'And what happens when you get bored?' Guy asked in a hard voice. 'There are no nightclubs round here, no convenient queue of boyfriends to take you out to dinner when you get sick of roast.'

'You've got a very exaggerated view of my social life,' Olivia told him. 'I had one boyfriend, yes, but he was hardly a queue.'

'And what about him? Is he coming out too?'

'He's just got married,' she said in an even tone. Guy's dark brows drew together. 'I see.'

'I doubt if you do.' Her eyes were a cold, clear green. 'Look, I'm sure it will be difficult for me to get used to, but I'm prepared to live without a social life for a while.' Turning abruptly away, she said, 'My parents died when I was not much older than David. I know how he feels.' She stared unseeingly at the tall, elegant gums shading the creek in the distance. Her voice was very low. 'Diane was my best friend then. She was always my best friend. Even when she married Pete and moved out here, we used to talk on the phone the whole time. She was always there when I needed her. Always there...' Her voice wobbled, but she finished steadily, 'I'm not leaving her son. That's all there is to it.'

'I see.' Guy was silent for so long that she turned slightly to look at him over her shoulder. He was watching her with an arrested expression, as if surprised by the unexpected glimpse of steel beneath the glamour. The flat planes of his face seemed to be accentuated by the shade. 'How long would you anticipate being my housekeeper?' he said at last in a dry voice.

'Two or three years? Until he goes away to school, I suppose.'

'It's not that easy, though, is it? You're just a tourist here. You can't just stay as long as you want—you won't get a visa to be a housekeeper. What's going to happen when your visa runs out?'

'I've thought of that,' Olivia said evenly. She took a deep breath. 'I'd like you to marry me.'

Silence. It stretched, twanged. Olivia was sure she could hear her words echoing around the outback, fading slowly into the distance. *Marry me. Marry me. Marry me.*

She could hear the wicker scrape protestingly against the wooden floorboards as Guy got to his feet. '*Marry* you?' he repeated softly. He was standing very close, the impression of leashed power almost overwhelming.

'Yes.' Olivia cleared her throat. 'The only way I could get a residency permit is to marry an Australian. It would be a strictly business arrangement,' she went on hurriedly, risking a glance at his inscrutable face. 'Just a formality, really. It would only need to be for a few years, as I said, and you'd save on a housekeeper's salary.' What else could she say to convince him? 'For David's sake...' she finished lamely.

Why didn't he say something? Unable to look at him directly, she was none the less acutely aware of him as he took his eyes from her face and leant his arms on the veranda rail. His stillness was unnerving. His gaze was fixed on the empty stockyards, where David's small figure could be seen hanging aimlessly over the wooden rails.

He wouldn't say anything until he had thought it through, Olivia realised resignedly, letting the calm of the afternoon settle on her as the tension slowly unwound into the silence. She hadn't realised quite how nervous she had been about approaching Guy, but now it was done. The decision was his.

'You're willing to do this for David?' he asked at last. 'Give up your career? Live in the outback? Marry a man you hardly know?'

'Yes.'

There was another long silence until, still looking out at the stockyards, he said, 'All right, I'll marry you—on two conditions.'

'Conditions?' Olivia tucked a swath of blonde hair behind her ear and eyed him warily.

'First, that it's just until David goes away to school.'

That was fair enough. There was no reason for him to want to tie himself to her for life, was there? She squashed a quite ridiculous feeling of hurt. 'What's the second condition?' she asked.

'That no one else knows the arrangement we've come to. As far as the rest of the world is concerned, we should be married like everyone else.'

She hesitated. 'That's not a problem, is it?'

'It's not a problem, no.' He looked up at her, his eyes creased against the light. 'But I wonder if you've thought about what it involves?'

'What do you mean?'

'We'll have to sleep together, for a start.'

For a long moment, Olivia couldn't say anything. Her heart did a long, slow somersault and thumped painfully back into place, as a vision of Guy making love to her presented itself with unnerving clarity. 'I——' Her voice sounded unnaturally high and she hastily cleared her throat. It wouldn't do to let Guy know how the idea had affected her. 'That won't be necessary, surely?' she managed stiffly.

The elusive amusement was lurking at the back of his eyes and around his mouth. 'Perhaps I should rephrase it? We'll have to share a room.'

'But I don't see why.'

'In Australia, most married couples share a room and a bed. Perhaps it's different in England?'

'Of course it's not!' She flushed at the sardonic note in his voice.

'Well, then.' Guy might have been discussing the price of feed, for all the emotion he showed, Olivia reflected bitterly. 'Look, Olivia, all I'm saying is that if we don't sleep in the same room pretty soon people are going to wonder what sort of marriage we have. You might think we're stuck out in the middle of nowhere, but I can assure you that everyone within a two-hundred-mile radius will know exactly what's going on everywhere else. Lots of people pass through a property like this—ringers, truckies, the vet, government inspectors, deliveries, roo shooters... You'd be surprised what they know.'

'So it's not as isolated as I thought.' Olivia tried to shrug carelessly. 'But what does it matter what they think?'

Guy's eyes shuttered. 'It matters to me, and it will matter to David. This is my home. I don't want people thinking there must be something wrong with me if my own wife won't sleep with me. And David—if he thinks we just got married for him, I think he'll feel guilty, even embarrassed. Do you want that?'

'No.' Olivia stepped away restlessly, pushing the silky hair away from her face in frustration. 'I didn't really have this in mind when I suggested marriage,' she said at last.

'I'm sure you didn't.' The dry amusement was unmistakable this time. 'You're the one who wants to get married. I'm just pointing out what it will entail. Quite apart from anything else, if the immigration authorities hear any gossip that leads them to suspect that ours isn't a real marriage you'll be out of Australia before you can bat those long eyelashes of yours. I think you should bear that in mind.'

Olivia folded her arms about her in agitation and began to pace up and down the veranda. 'All right, all right. Point taken. It's not as straightforward as I thought it was.' She paused, and turned back to face him, biting her lip. 'I suppose we ought to be honest about this. What exactly do you expect out of this marriage?'

Guy raised one eyebrow, and Olivia found herself noticing the texture of his skin, the way the brown hair grew at his temples. She had a sudden urge to reach out and run her fingers over his jaw to feel the first faint prickle of stubble.

'Just what we've discussed.' She jerked her attention back to what he was saying. 'David's a responsibility that we share. I expect you to be a mother for David, and a housekeeper for me. I also expect you to behave like any other affectionate wife—at least when anyone else is present.'

'Then sharing a room isn't...' Olivia found herself floundering. 'When you said sleep together, did you mean...would you expect...?' Damn him! Why didn't he help her? He must know quite well what she meant! 'Will you ... I mean, will *we* ...?' She trailed off to look at him hopelessly.

Guy looked back, expressionless.

'Not until you ask, Olivia.'

\*     \*     \*

Later, Olivia could remember almost nothing about her wedding—only Guy pushing the ring impersonally on to her finger, and looking down at her name in the register with something like a shock. Olivia Bridewell, successful career woman, was now Olivia Richardson, a wife, but not a real wife. A mother, but not a real mother.

It had taken her ages to decide what to wear. She didn't want Guy to think she was making a big deal of the ceremony, but it was her wedding, after all, and it would look odd if she made no effort at all. In the end she'd chosen a suit in wild sandalwood silk. It was very plain, with a short, round-necked jacket and a narrow skirt, but it was one of her favourite outfits. She had often worn it for business lunches, or important meetings. It made her feel cool, feminine, confident.

She needed all the confidence she could get today, she'd thought, fastening a flat gold link necklace around her neck. At the last moment she changed her earrings for a pair of silver dolphins. They didn't really go, but Diane had given them to her. Today, of all days, she wanted to remember Diane. She'd touched them as if they were a talisman as she inspected her solemn reflection in the mirror.

'I hope I'm doing the right thing, Diane,' she'd whispered.

Guy had casually announced that they were going into Cloncurry to get married that morning, and the ringers had been too polite, or too uninterested, to ask awkward questions about the reasons for such a sudden, businesslike wedding. They had mumbled congratulations, reassuring each other that it would be good to have a woman at Willagong Creek—as if any woman would have done, Olivia thought in exasperation.

David had said only, 'Oh, so you're staying,' but she had seen a flash of relief in his eyes, and it was enough to strengthen her resolve.

Now, staring out of the window as they drove back along the bumpy track to Willagong Creek, she twisted the ring on her finger and thought about Guy. Her husband. It irritated her that she could remember vividly every time he had touched her, however brief and impersonal. What would it be like lying in bed next to that lean, hard body? What would it be like if he turned towards her and touched her, not impersonally, but intimately, letting his hands linger against her skin...

Not until you ask, Olivia.

Olivia's eyes snapped green at the memory. If he thought she was going to beg him to make love to her, he had another think coming! She wouldn't so much as ask him to take the lid off a jamjar for her!

Reassured by the rush of angry pride, she tilted her chin at the still, silent landscape. She had reluctantly agreed to share a room with Guy, but he should not have the satisfaction of knowing that it bothered her one little bit! She would be very cool, very sophisticated, and with any luck *he* would be the one to feel uncomfortable!

She stole a covert glance at him under her lashes. His hands were relaxed, competent on the steering-wheel, his eyes scanning the horizon, noting the dryness, checking the fences, assessing the condition of the cattle. He was clearly *not* wasting any time wondering about climbing into bed next to her!

No, Guy was not going to be the one who felt uncomfortable. Olivia looked away with a tiny sigh. He must feel *something*. Would he be wishing he was in bed with someone else? What about the elusive girlfriend that David had talked about? Guy had never mentioned her, and surely if she had been serious he wouldn't even have considered Olivia's offer...

'Why have you never married before?' she asked abruptly.

He glanced at her, then back at the horizon. 'Never got round to it. I've thought about it, lots of times. A place like this needs a woman—as you've noticed. I guess I haven't had time to find myself a suitable girl.'

'So now you've ended up with an unsuitable one?'

He glanced at her again, and this time his eyes lingered on her warm flawless skin, on the swinging hair, dramatic sea-blue eyes and elegant suit. 'Ye-es,' he agreed slowly. There was a tantalising almost-smile lurking in his eyes and about his mouth.

Olivia felt something deep inside her clench. 'Won't the ringers think it funny that you married someone so unsuitable?' she asked defensively.

'Why should they? You're an attractive girl, as
you're well aware. I should think they'll probably
draw their own conclusions.'

Guy's voice was dry, and Olivia flushed. 'Perhaps
people might think it's odd that I married *you*?'
she said, more sharply than she had intended.

'That's more likely,' he agreed equably. Another
amused glance. 'You'll just have to convince anyone
who asks that you're madly in love with me.'

'That's hardly likely!' she snapped, unaccountably ruffled.

'As the saying goes, I know that, you know that,
but they don't know that. And, more importantly,
the immigration authorities don't know that.'

Olivia bit her lip, silenced by his cool reminder
of the reason for their marriage.

After a while, he asked, 'What about you?'

'Me?'

'How come you're not married? You must be,
what, thirty?'

'Twenty-nine,' Olivia said icily.

Guy shrugged, unapologetic. 'Twenty-nine,
then.'

'I suppose I never got round to it either,' she said
after a pause. 'I went out with Tim for years. We
talked about it every now and then, but I had my
career and Tim had his, and...I don't know...there
didn't seem to be any need to make such a big com-
mitment. We worked for the same organisation, so
we saw each other the whole time.' She sighed. 'I
suppose we stayed together out of habit more than
anything else. If it had been a real relationship, we

would never have hesitated so long. It certainly didn't take Tim long to commit himself once he met Linda.'

She was unaware of the note of bitterness in her voice, but Guy glanced at her. 'So you've come all the way to Australia to get over your broken heart?' he said sardonically. 'Is marriage to me just part of your revenge on this Tim?'

'I married you for the same reason that I came to Australia—David,' Olivia reminded him coldly. 'I'm not denying that it was a welcome opportunity to get away from things, but if you think I would marry someone like you for a petty reason like pique you're much mistaken!'

'So, what's he like—Tim?'

Olivia gave a little shrug. 'Very sociable. Lots of fun. Successful.' For the first time she realised that she couldn't conjure up a clear picture of Tim's face. His memory seemed blurred, like that of someone she had known years ago.

'Sounds more your type,' Guy commented, and Olivia wondered if she could possibly have imagined an undercurrent of jealousy in his voice. But his face was as unrevealing as ever, and she turned back to the window, deciding that she must have been mistaken.

'Yes, I suppose he is.'

They finished the journey in silence.

# CHAPTER FOUR

THE homestead was deserted when they arrived, and Guy lost no time in changing back into jeans and boots and dark cotton shirt. He disappeared in the direction of the stockyards, leaving Olivia alone with the silent, dusty house.

My wedding-day, she thought sadly, running a finger along a shelf and leaving a deep groove in the dust. Until Linda had come on the scene, she had always imagined herself marrying Tim in some vague future. Tim was a traditionalist; there would have been a church, cake, tossing the bouquet. She closed her eyes, trying to imagine the scene, but all she could see was Guy's face, the elusive amusement and the deep creases round his eyes before he turned back to squint at the horizon once more.

As if drawn, she walked slowly down the corridor and opened the door to Guy's room. *Their* room. The vast iron bedstead faced the windows, dominating the room. *Their* bed. Olivia stood at the foot and stared down at it, chewing her lip uncertainly. Did Guy really expect her to calmly climb in next to him? What if she found herself rolling against him, skin against skin? What then? Involuntarily, she shivered.

She couldn't do it! Wrapping her arms tightly round her in a characteristic gesture, she moved abruptly away to the window. She was nervous, and resentful of the fact. She had always been in control before, of her job, her men, her life. It wasn't the thought of Guy touching her that unnerved her, it was the knowledge that she might not be able to control her own reactions if he did.

Her sense of resentment grew as she dragged her cases along the corridor and unpacked. She didn't want Guy to make her feel unsettled and jittery. She wanted to feel coolly sophisticated again; sleeping with Guy was just part of the deal. And while it might be just a business arrangement, he could at least have spent the afternoon with her on their wedding-day. He was the one who was so keen for it to look like a normal marriage, after all!

Her clothes looked all wrong hanging in the wardrobe next to Guy's. Olivia viewed them moodily. On top of the chest of drawers, her cosmetics were bright splashes of colour and frivolity, out of place in the plain masculine room.

The sandalwood suit was crushed and grubby after the long drive. Guy hadn't commented on it once, she realised as she stripped it off and showered.

Convincing herself that she didn't care, Olivia changed into a soft, floaty dress in mingled blues and greens which deepened the blue of her eyes. It was strange how comforting familiar routines were, she thought, automatically applying subtle make-up, and searching through her things for a matching pair of shoes. When she had finished, she felt more like herself again.

She found Guy out on the veranda as usual, sitting relaxed in one of the wicker chairs, a can of beer on the floor by his side. Not for the first time, Olivia wished there was some music, anything to detract from the empty silence. It never seemed to bother Guy. He unfolded his lean frame from the chair as she appeared, raising one eyebrow in typically understated surprise.

'You've changed.' His dark eyes swept over her, and to her chagrin Olivia immediately found some of her newly regained composure slipping away.

'Very perceptive of you,' she said snippily. 'I didn't think you noticed what I wore.'

'What makes you say that?'

'I might as well have been wearing a sack today for all the notice you took!'

'I noticed all right.' A look of amusement crossed Guy's face. 'I just thought brown was a funny colour to choose to wear to a wedding.'

'It wasn't brown, it was sandalwood,' Olivia corrected him, tight-lipped.

'Looked brown to me.' The amusement deepened, but the smile remained infuriatingly elusive.

'Well, it wasn't!' Why was she arguing about it? she wondered, cross with herself as much as with him.

He shrugged. 'You're the fashion expert.' He resumed his seat. 'You planning to change for dinner every night?'

'I usually do.' She stiffened at the implied criticism in his voice. 'It wouldn't do the rest of you any harm to change either. It would set a good example to David.'

Guy took a long pull at his beer, regarding her thoughtfully over the top of his can. 'Going to lick us all into shape, are you, Olivia?'

'I don't think I'm likely to have much success somehow.' Her voice was edged with bitterness as she lowered herself warily on to the other sagging chair.

'Why not? We're not as stuck in our ways as you seem to think.'

'Aren't you? I can just imagine the fuss if I tried to change anything!'

Guy's eyes rested on the flawless profile. 'Somehow I think you're going to change things just by being here, Olivia.'

She glanced at him quickly, surprised by the odd note in his voice, but the deep brown eyes gave nothing away. He was like the land, she thought, hard and brown and uncompromising, and without warning the image of lying in bed next to him recurred so vividly that she caught her breath at her own alarming twist of reaction.

'What's the matter?' He was watching her more closely than she realised and had seen her involuntary gasp.

'Nothing,' she said quickly. She must get a hold of herself! She got up again and walked to the rail.

'You seem nervous,' he commented.

'Nervous? What have I got to be nervous about?'

'That's what I'm wondering.' Guy finished his beer and stood up too. 'Afraid I'm going to jump on you?'

'Of course not!' she lied. She wished fervently that he didn't seem to possess that uncanny ability to read her mind. She lifted her chin. 'Anyway, you've made it more than clear that it's the last thing on your mind.'

'I wouldn't say that,' he said, a glimmer of amusement back in his eyes.

'Oh? I was under the distinct impression that you didn't even notice I was there today, despite the fact that we were getting married! You made no effort to be pleasant, and you've ignored me ever since we got back!'

'You're not the kind of girl that doesn't get noticed, Olivia, and you know it.' Guy's voice was deep and slow, and suddenly he was standing very close. She had her back to the veranda rail, dimly aware of the wood pressing into her as she watched, half mesmerised, his hand reach out and push her hair gently away from her face. 'I'm not ignoring you now,' he said.

His fingers were strong against the softness of her cheek. A thrill of awareness shivered through her, as if every fibre of her was responding to his touch. Her mind told her to tear her eyes away from his face, move away from the disturbing excitement of his nearness, but her body refused to move, and then the opportunity was gone as he cupped her face in both hands and bent his head to kiss her.

At the first touch of his lips, Olivia's mental resistance shattered in an explosion of giddy delight. It was as if she had always known it would be like this, as if every second since he had turned and walked towards her in that Townsville hotel had arrowed into this moment when all that mattered was his cool, firm mouth and the dizzying rush of sensation through her veins.

Instinctively, she leant into him, her lips warm and inviting beneath his, her hands lifting of their own accord to his chest. Guy's fingers tightened against her face, then relaxed to slide down through her silky hair to her throat. His thumbs were hard and calloused, just as she'd imagined, as he ran them caressingly along the pure line of her jaw, and she quivered with exquisite awareness, felt herself melting in a flame of passion which ran between them, burning higher and higher until it was out of their control.

Guy's hands were hard, almost rough, against the soft material of her dress as he pulled her closer, and she clutched at him, aware only of a need to feel him closer still——

'Yuk! Kissing!' David's disgusted voice jerked them apart like a douse of cold water. He was watching them from the steps, with a small boy's scorn for a pointless pastime.

Olivia fell back against the veranda rail as Guy released her, her eyes dark blue with arousal, and wide with the shock of the sickeningly abrupt return to reality.

'What were you doing that for?' David went on accusingly to Guy, who appeared to have himself under much better control.

He didn't even look at Olivia as he moved away. 'We're married,' he said to David. 'Kissing's the reason people get married, isn't it, Olivia?'

Olivia swallowed, so horrified at her response to Guy's kiss that she could hardly speak. 'One of the reasons,' she managed, in a thin, high voice.

David was unconvinced, and clearly disappointed in Guy's betrayal of manliness. 'I came to tell you supper was ready,' he said.

Olivia's knees were so weak that she wondered how she would ever be able to walk over to the cookhouse, but somehow she managed it, and sat in a daze while Guy talked to the ringers as if nothing had happened.

How could he behave so normally? she thought furiously. *His* heart obviously wasn't pounding, his mind wasn't in a whirl of confused emotions, as hers was, where exhilaration fought with dismay at her own reaction, bitter disappointment with relief at David's interruption.

She stared down at her plate. She'd been kissed before, had enjoyed being kissed, but no man had ever kissed her with such devastating effect. She had always been in control before, and it was humiliating to realise how utterly she had abandoned herself—and to Guy Richardson, of all people! A man who hardly noticed her, a man who didn't even like her, a man who could calmly sit there discussing *cows* while she was still aflame with his touch.

'Olivia?'

Olivia started at the sound of her own name. 'Sorry?' David was looking at her enquiringly.

'Her mind's on other things,' Ben teased, with a knowing wink at Darren. 'Being her wedding night...'

'What difference does that make?' David asked, mystified by the wink and the fiery blush that had spread over Olivia's face.

'David wanted to know if you were going to learn how to ride now that you're staying,' Guy interrupted easily.

Furious with herself for her girlish blush, and with Ben for guessing so unerringly, and so tactlessly, what was on her mind, Olivia pulled herself together. 'I don't think so,' she said in what she hoped was a cool way.

'You ought to ride.' Corky made a surprising entry into the conversation. 'All the Willagong women have been able to ride.'

'Not this Willagong woman,' Olivia said firmly. 'I'll drive.'

'You won't get very far in a vehicle round here,' said Guy. 'Corky's right; the women here have all ridden, because they needed to ride.'

'I won't need a horse to do the cooking or the cleaning,' she snapped. 'And judging by the state of things round here, I won't have time to do anything else!'

'You could come with me and Guy when we go riding in the evenings,' David offered. 'Couldn't she, Guy?'

'If she wanted to.' Guy's eyes held that familiar, lurking gleam of amusement. 'You're not frightened of horses as well as spiders, are you, Olivia?'

Terrified would be closer to the mark. 'No,' said Olivia haughtily. Her pride had taken enough of a battering this evening, without admitting that too, and she was relieved when the discussion turned to horses and which would be the gentlest for her to start on. They only ever seemed to become animated when they were talking about horses or cattle. Olivia had no intention of riding. She would find a better excuse when the time came; for now it would take all her concentration not to think about later, when she would have to get into bed next to Guy.

If only he hadn't kissed her. If only she didn't have to lie next to him and remember the feel of his lips and the taut strength of his body against hers. If only she had never asked him to marry her. She ploughed through the meal without tasting any of it. After her embarrassingly eager response to his kiss, Guy would think she was some kind of sex-starved nymphomaniac. She would have to make it very clear to him that it had been no more than an aberration, or he would think that every time she moved in bed she was about to throw herself at him. Olivia's pride balked at the thought.

He had taken her unawares, but it wouldn't happen again.

It seemed that the meal would never end, but at last she used David as an excuse to slip away, and leave Guy and the men still talking about horses. He probably didn't even notice she'd gone, she thought bitterly, undressing with jerkily nervous gestures. She was of a lot less interest than an animal as far as Guy Richardson was concerned!

'Good!' she said out loud as if to convince herself.

In the daylight it had been an enormous bed, but now it seemed to have shrunk alarmingly. They would never be able to avoid touching each other. Olivia walked fretfully around the room, trying to persuade herself that it was no big deal.

'So what if you do brush against him?' she asked her reflection. 'He's not interested in you. You're not interested in him. Just move away and go back to sleep. No problem.' Her reflection looked a little more confident. No problem.

If she had known that she was going to end up sharing a bed with Guy Richardson, she would have bought herself a nightdress before she came out, she reflected. She hadn't worn one for years, but there was no way she was going to lie next to Guy with no clothes on! In the end she had found a baggy T-shirt to wear, but it felt hot and constricting as she threw back the blanket and slipped gingerly between the sheets.

She lay rigid, willing herself to be asleep before Guy came in. The moonlight was bright in the room, but it was a hot night and to close the shutters would certainly be too stuffy. She wriggled in her T-shirt and punched her pillow into a more comfortable shape. She would never be able to sleep.

Her stomach was knotted with apprehension, her mouth dry. She longed more than anything else for this night to be over. Think about David, she told herself sternly. Think about Diane. Think about anything except Guy's hands against your skin.

When the door opened softly, the breath seemed to freeze in her lungs. Squeezing her eyes tight, she lay still and pretended to be asleep, acutely aware of the sounds of Guy moving around the room. She could hear the quiet thud of his boots hitting the floor, the clunk as the metal on his belt knocked against the wooden chair. Then there was the unmistakable sound of unzipping jeans, and a subdued rustle as he removed the rest of his clothes.

Olivia, her eyes screwed shut, could visualise it all as clearly as if he had stripped in broad daylight, and her pulse began to thud so loudly that she was sure Guy must be able to hear it too.

The bed creaked and sagged. She held her breath.

'There's no need to panic,' Guy said into the darkness.

She said nothing, hoping he would think that she was really asleep. She tried to breathe deeply and evenly, but it was hard when every sense was screaming awareness of the body lying so close beside her.

'I know you're not asleep,' he said conversationally, and then, when she still didn't reply, reached out to run a finger down her spine. Olivia flinched, unable to prevent a gasp of reaction. 'I didn't think you were asleep,' he said, a dry edge to his voice.

'I'm trying to sleep,' she muttered into her pillow. 'I'm very tired.'

The next moment she found herself pulled roughly over on to her back to lie staring wide-eyed with shock up at Guy looming above her. 'I'm tired too,' he said. 'Too tired to play games. I'm not going to sleep every night with you quaking on the other side of the bed, so I think we should get this straight now. If you think I'm overcome with desire at the thought of going to bed with you, you can think again, Olivia. I'm not interested in a woman who wishes she was in bed with another man. Don't bother to deny it,' he added, as she opened her mouth to protest. 'I can tell that you're still in love with this Tim bloke, and you can keep yourself warm with dreams of him as far as I'm concerned. I've already told you I won't touch you unless you ask.'

'I didn't ask on the veranda!' Olivia's eyes gleamed defiantly up at his in the moonlight.

'Didn't you? Seemed to me those eyes of yours were asking me pretty clearly, and I didn't notice you pushing me away. Quite the opposite, in fact.'

'You took me by surprise,' she said furiously, lashing out in anger and wounded pride. 'And if you think I enjoyed being kissed like that, *you* can think again! Your cowboy technique might go down very well with the girls out here, but I'm used to a rather more sophisticated approach!'

Guy's eyes narrowed. 'Oh, so Tim's sophisticated, is he, as well as being sociable and successful and such fun?'

'Yes, he is!' Olivia was too angry to put him right about her feelings for Tim. She had been fond of him, and was hurt when he left her, but she had put him firmly behind her when she came out to Australia.

'Well, I may not be as sophisticated as Tim, but even I can tell when a woman is enjoying being kissed or not! You just didn't like the fact that you enjoyed the...what was it you called it?...the cowboy technique.' Shifting abruptly to pin her beneath him, he held her wrists in a hard grip away from her body. 'Too unsophisticated for you, was it, Olivia?'

Olivia was trembling with a mixture of anger, panic and treacherous arousal. 'Yes!' she said bravely, knowing even as he lowered his head that it was too late.

His mouth was warmer, more persuasive than before. His hands held her arms still, and there was only the heat of their bodies and the touch of their lips. Expecting him to be rough and angry, Olivia was unprepared for the gentleness which crept insidiously beneath her defences, leaving her open and vulnerable to the glow of excitement that began to flicker and then flame.

She hardly noticed when he released her wrists, and ran his hands over the slender lines of her body, slipping beneath the T-shirt to burn against her skin. His lips explored the sensitive hollow below her ear, whispered down her throat, and she murmured low with indistinct pleasure, arching her body instinctively to his touch, arms sliding of their own volition about his neck.

Guy was drawing away. Olivia lifted languid eyelids to encounter a blaze of expression in his eyes, but, before she had time to decipher it, they shuttered and she was left staring into opaque depths.

'You might get used to the cowboy technique, Olivia,' he said, the coolness of his voice as shocking as a slap in the face. 'You might even find you get to like it.'

'That wasn't fair,' she whispered.

'It wasn't gentlemanly, was it? But then I'm a cowboy, not a gentleman, and I don't think you're quite such a lady as you like to think. Comfort yourself with the memory of your precious Tim if that's what you want, Olivia, but if you need...what shall I say to avoid hurting those sophisticated feelings of yours?...a physical relationship, then you only have to ask.'

She was shaking, glad of the rush of fury that surged through her at his callous words. She knew she had provoked him with her comment about cowboys, and if she hadn't known better she might have suspected jealousy, but her pride was badly dented by the way he seemed so unmoved by her, and, instead of talking sensibly like the cool, well-balanced adult she was supposed to be, she moved ostentatiously back to the very edge of the bed. 'Don't hold your breath!' she said bitterly. Her only—faint—hope was to try and appear as un-affected as he was by those giddy moments of pleasure.

'I won't,' he said. 'As long as you stop lying there as if you're about to be offered up for sacrifice.' He turned his back on her, and settled for sleep. 'Breakfast is at six. You'll need to be up at five-thirty.'

# CHAPTER FIVE

OLIVIA sat at the scrubbed table, cradling a mug of coffee, and contemplated making a cake without enthusiasm. She had never enjoyed baking—airy soufflés and subtle sauces were more her style— and the sun streaming in through the cookhouse windows only served to emphasise the grimy kitchen. She would have to clean everything before she could even start.

It was only eight o'clock and she felt as if she had been up for hours. Guy and the ringers had eaten their steaks in taciturn silence and disappeared before seven. 'Make the boys something for smoko, will you?' Guy had said, settling his hat on his head.

'Smoko?' she queried blankly.

'Mid-morning tea and something solid to eat,' he explained briefly. 'We'll be back at ten.'

She had nodded, still unable to look at him directly this morning. Last night's kiss, the seeping excitement and bitter anger, had settled into embarrassment and determination never to provoke such a scene again. This morning she had wanted to run straight back to London and never have to face Guy again, but of course she couldn't. There was David to think of. She had been ridiculously nervous yesterday and her behaviour had been out

of character: from now on she would be cool and
businesslike, and keep her part of the deal with
Guy—for David's sake, if not for her own peace
of mind.

In the meantime, she had better just get on with
it. Olivia got to her feet and looked around the
kitchen rather doubtfully. If only there was a radio,
some music, any kind of noise to cut through the
silence! Her whole life in London had revolved
around music. She had spent her days discussing
programmes, and the evenings, when Guy imagined her dancing away in some steamy nightclub,
had more often than not been spent at classical
concerts, or with musician friends who would end
up talking, playing or improvising music into the
early hours of the morning.

Looking back, her days and nights had been
played to a continuous soundtrack of music. She
liked pop music as well, and would listen to the
radio while she drank her morning coffee. There
would be a cassette in the car on the way to the
office, music in the shops, music in the restaurants.
After Tim had announced his engagement to Linda,
after Diane had died, Olivia had spent long evenings lying on the sofa and letting the pure notes
of Mozart or Dvorak wash over her in soothing
comfort.

Never before had she wished so much that she
could play an instrument herself. Then at least she
would have been able to make her own music, but
she had long ago had to accept that she had no
talent for it, and that the closest she could get to

the music world was as an administrator. At Willagong Creek she wouldn't even be able to talk about music, and the only music she would have to work by would be her own tuneless humming.

By ten o'clock she was hot, sticky and covered in dirt and grime from cleaning the cupboards. It was easier to clean than to think about Guy, and she had scrubbed furiously, as if she could as easily scrub away the memory of his kiss and her own humiliating response.

She rose stiffly to her feet as the ringers came in, taking off their hats and stamping the worst of the dust off their boots.

Wiping the sweat off her upper lip with her arm, she said, 'I'll put the kettle on.' Why were they all looking so surprised? she wondered crossly, unaware of the drastic change in her appearance. At breakfast she had been coolly elegant; now she was hot and bothered, the shining hair clinging to her neck and forehead, the pale, expensive shirt stained and grubby, the trousers damp and crumpled.

'I'll do it, Mrs R,' Joe said.

Mrs R? Olivia looked blank, then realised that he was addressing her. 'Oh, thank you, J——' She stopped as Guy came in, letting the screen door bang behind him. It was odd the way he seemed to dominate the room. Joe was taller, Ben was better-looking, but only Guy could stop the breath in her throat just by standing there. The sleeves of his blue workshirt were rolled up and she could could see a light film of dust on the dark hairs of his forearms.

He took off his hat and rubbed a hand over his jaw as if to wipe off the worst of the dust there.

Only now did Olivia realise what a sight she must look, and she began to brush ineffectually at the grime on her arms. 'I was just doing some cleaning,' she said.

'So I see.' Secret amusement crinkled his eyes.

Olivia found herself willing him to smile at her, but he only turned away and sat down at the table with the others. She was taken aback by her stab of disappointment, and vexation with herself sharpened her voice to brittle Englishness.

'Coffee, everyone?'

'Tea,' said Guy firmly. 'We only have coffee after supper.'

Olivia's lips tightened. She made some tea in a big, battered metal pot and then very deliberately poured herself a coffee. Risking a glance at Guy, she saw he was well aware of her reaction, and she put down her cup with a hand that was suddenly unsteady. She could make all the resolutions she liked about staying cool and businesslike with Guy, but he only had to walk in the room to have her acting jittery and illogical again.

She looked at him again. The dust on his face gave his skin a matt appearance, and the lean lines of cheek and jaw were very pronounced. His brown eyes were shrewd, amused. Why didn't he smile?

'I see you've been baking too,' he remarked.

Olivia flushed. The cake sat on a wire rack, hard and flat, an admission of failure. She had tried to salvage it with icing, but somehow it had only made it look worse. After all she had had to say about Corky's cooking, it was a humiliating start.

'It would have helped to have had some decent equipment,' she said defensively. 'It's bad enough making a cake at the best of times, without having to guess at all the quantities and temperatures.'

'I thought you were a cordon bleu cook?' he said, with deceptive innocence.

'I am.' Olivia gritted her teeth. 'I'm just a little rusty on baking.'

Guy was unsympathetic. 'You'll get used to it.'

Like his kisses? Her eyes slid away from his, remembering his comments last night. 'The kitchen needs to be completely cleaned and restocked,' she said quickly. 'When can I go shopping?'

'Shopping?' He looked at her as if she'd asked to go to the moon. 'There's a whole roomful of goods out there in the cold store. You'll have to make do with what we've got.'

Olivia had glanced in the store earlier and had been unimpressed by its shelves stocked high with basics like tins of powdered milk, sugar and flour. In the huge walk-in fridge she had found a dull selection of vegetables and enormous haunches of freshly butchered beef that made her wrinkle her nose in distaste. Why had she never appreciated the supermarket at home with its range of exotic fruit and vegetables and meat wrapped in nice, sanitised plastic packages?

'It's not exactly an inspirational choice,' she pointed out, thinking that even a few herbs and spices would liven things up a bit.

'We don't need inspiration,' Guy said flatly. 'All we need is plain, nourishing food, and you can do that perfectly well with what's here. I'm flying to Townsville next week, so if we're running short of anything I can stock up then. You might make a list.'

'Townsville?' Olivia brightened at the reassuring thought of a city. 'Can I come?'

'No.'

'But why not?' She still couldn't get used to such abrupt refusal from a man.

The ringers were talking among themselves at the far end of the table and tucking into the cake with every evidence of enjoyment—they didn't have the most discerning of palates, Olivia reflected irrelevantly—but Guy leaned closer so that only she could hear. His mouth was set in a stern line. 'You claimed that you wanted to look after David, Olivia, and that's what you're going to do. That means staying here with him, not jaunting off on shopping trips.'

'It's all right for you to go jaunting off, though!' Olivia pointed out rebelliously, unsettled by his nearness and determined not to show it.

'I've got a property to run. There are times when I have to be away, otherwise I wouldn't have needed a woman to look after David.'

A woman, any old woman! Olivia's eyes sparkled dangerously green, but she bit back the bitter retort that sprang to her lips. Cool, businesslike, that was her. 'Where can I buy the things I need now?' she asked in a reasonable tone.

'Like what?'

'Well...' She searched her mind feverishly. 'I need some eggs. I used the last two in the cake.'

Guy looked long-suffering. 'Eggs? Even a city girl like you must know where eggs come from!' He nodded his head towards the door. 'I'm afraid you're going to have to resign yourself to a shopless existence from now on, Olivia. You'll find the chooks in a run across from the ringers' quarters.'

Draining his mug, he stood up. 'We'd better get back to work. Lunch at one o'clock, please.'

'Yes, sir!' Olivia muttered, left staring resentfully at where the screen door banged into place after the last man.

With a sigh, she leant her elbows on the table and propped her forehead in her hands. No music, no company, no shops, no relief from the endless round of cleaning and meals. How was she going to stand it?

If she had been in London she would have been dictating letters, translating programme notes, sending off telexes, gossiping over coffee, worrying about how to get a hundred musicians and all their instruments from Rome to Berlin, rushing off to meet record producers, taking a call from the BBC while she was putting on her coat and talking to the promoter in Japan at the same time... It had taken her a long time to prove to her boss that she was just as good as Tim and should be made a director as well, but she had loved every minute—until Tim had decided he wanted to marry his secretary, a pretty girl whose ambitions went only as far as a house and family.

Olivia was sure that Tim had come to resent her own success, and she didn't blame him for wanting to marry someone who would be less of a challenge. The only thing she hated was the fact that everybody knew. She hated the sympathetic looks, the disbelief when she smiled and said she didn't care, and it had been a relief to head for a country where nobody knew her for a while. She had planned to go back, of course, to show them all that she could make a success of her own business, but those plans had had to be shelved for a while. She had no business to run at Willagong Creek, only a house to clean and six stomachs to be filled.

It was an unexciting prospect, but she would bear it. She would have to.

She was still sitting there when the creak of the screen door made her look up, expecting David, who had disappeared clutching jamjars after breakfast, no doubt in search of insects.

It was Guy. He stood for a moment looking down at the unguarded expression in her turquoise eyes. 'You'd better wear this for cleaning,' he said abruptly, tossing one of his shirts on to the table. 'I daresay it won't co-ordinate with your trousers, but it'll save you ruining any more of your clothes.'

He turned on his heel and left before Olivia had time to recover from her surprise. She would have thought he'd consider her expensive clothes merely unsuitable, and that he would simply shrug off any damage as her own fault for having nothing better to wear.

She pulled the shirt towards her. It was a little frayed round the collar and cuffs, and the blue and green checked cotton was soft with age. There was no doubt it would be more comfortable than her own shirt, which clung damply to her back.

Peeling it off, she shrugged herself into Guy's shirt, smoothing it down with slightly hesitant hands. The material was cool and comfortable against her skin; it smelt clean and sun-dried, with a lingering, indefinable male scent.

Guy's shirt. For no reason, Olivia felt a flush spread slowly over her body at the thought of wearing his clothes against her bare skin. It seemed suddenly very intimate, and she was uncomfortably aware of her nakedness beneath the shirt. It was almost as if he were touching her himself...

'Don't be ridiculous!' she said out loud. 'It's an old shirt, that's all.'

She walked slowly over to the chicken run, trying not to think about the way the material brushed against her as if in intimate caresses as she moved. The hens rushed over to greet her as she let herself into the run, flapping their wings ridiculously and tumbling over themselves in their eagerness to find out what scraps she had brought.

'I haven't got anything,' she confessed, feeling absurdly guilty as they clucked hopefully around her feet. She was a failure as far as the chickens were concerned too! 'I'll bring you some scraps later.'

She found almost a dozen eggs in the roost and carried them back gathered in the front of Guy's shirt. They were dirtier than she was used to seeing in the shops, so she washed them and laid them out neatly, then wished she hadn't. Guy would only sneer.

Determined to prove that she could cook, Olivia used some of the eggs to make a magnificent quiche for lunch, but that turned out to be the wrong thing too.

'You don't need to bother cooking anything for lunch,' Guy said briskly. 'Meat and bread and salad, that's all they need.'

The arrival of Ben and Darren, clattering up the steps, effectively silenced Olivia's protests. Her beautiful quiche, spurned for tough, grey meat! He might at least have said how nice it looked, she thought, slicing beef sullenly.

She could see Ben and Darren eyeing the quiche and the perfectly arranged salad out of the corner of their eyes, and exchanging glances with Corky and Joe as they arrived in their turn. David arrived last, looking grubby.

'Ugh—quiche! Yeuch!' He screwed up his face in disgust as he spotted Olivia's work of art, lacking the inhibitions that had obviously kept the ringers from saying exactly the same thing.

'That's enough, David.' Guy's quiet voice stopped David in his tracks.

'Sorry,' he muttered in Olivia's direction.

She sighed, defeated. 'Don't worry,' she said resignedly. 'There's bread and meat as well, and I promise never to make the salad look nice again!'

There were a few sheepish smiles as they all sat down. As if to atone for their lack of enthusiasm, the ringers each took a tiny slice of quiche, and ate it stolidly, but with such an air of self-sacrifice that Olivia wished they hadn't bothered. Guy took a large piece, she noticed, but ate it without comment.

Her mind began to wander as the men talked about mending fences and checking licks, whatever licks were. There was a little restaurant she knew in Strasbourg, where they served the best quiche lorraine she had ever tasted, but the one she had made that morning was nearly as good. It was fortunate they had a more appreciative audience in Strasbourg...

'Is that Guy's shirt you're wearing, Mrs R?'

Olivia started to find herself addressed directly. 'Er—yes...yes, it is.'

'Thought I recognised it,' Ben said to Corky with satisfaction. 'That's the shirt he wears the whole time.'

'So it is.' Corky looked closer at Olivia, who sat feeling absurdly self-conscious at the end of the table, and added surprisingly, 'Looks better on Mrs R, though, doesn't it, Guy?'

There was a pause. Almost shyly, Olivia looked down the table to where Guy sat opposite her. Had he really given her his favourite shirt? His dark eyes were unreadable, his face expressionless as ever, but illogically she found herself remembering how he had kissed her in vivid detail. The memory brought a warm tide of colour to her cheeks, and she looked quickly down at her plate.

'Yes,' said Guy, 'it does.'

David regarded Olivia critically. 'You don't look as smart as you usually do,' he observed, with small-boy candour. He crammed the last of his bread into his mouth and continued indistinctly, 'Did you choose it specially? It's the same colour as your eyes. Look, Guy!'

Olivia risked another fleeting glance at Guy. He was still watching her, and she felt oddly breathless.

'Exactly the same colour,' he agreed calmly.

He had said nothing, done nothing. So why was her heart thudding uncomfortably against her ribs? Why had her appetite deserted her? Olivia pushed the remains of her quiche irritably around her plate. She had already decided not to let Guy affect her any more. *She* was the one who was cool and so-phisticated round here. *She* was the one who could set pulses racing with a smile. Not Guy Richardson with his infuriatingly unreadable eyes, Guy who didn't even smile. It was stupid to speculate about his shirt, pointless to analyse the little thrill of pleasure to know that he'd actually noticed the colour of her eyes.

Left alone with the dishes and the chaotic kitchen once more, Olivia threw herself into cleaning in an effort to take her mind off all those things about Guy she had decided not to think about, but by three o'clock she was sick of it. Turning her back on damp cloths and scrubbing brushes, she closed the cookhouse door behind her and headed off, with no clear idea of where she was going as long as it was away from the homestead.

The glare hit her as she stepped outside, making her screw up her eyes, and the heat bounced off the dry ground. She waved the flies away from her face and hesitated by the stockyards, where the track forked. To the left it stretched straight to the horizon, through interminable, shimmering scrub. To the right, past the paddock where the horses brooded in the shade, lay the creek.

Shading her eyes against the sun, Olivia chose the creek. She slithered down the banks to walk along the river bed, completely dry now after months without rain. Desiccated brown gum leaves rustled beneath her feet, filling the air with their sun-dried fragrance. It was almost eerily quiet.

She wandered aimlessly, scuffing through the leaves every now and then. It had been a humiliating morning. She had always been a perfectionist, and it irritated her that she had not been able to demonstrate to Guy quite how capable and efficient she was. He would think her totally inadequate after this morning, she realised glumly. Her clothes were wrong, her cooking was wrong, *she* was wrong.

Crushing a few of the narrow gum leaves in her hand, she bent to breathe in their scent before letting the dried fragments crumble through her fingers. This was her life now. She would have to prove to Guy that she could do things right too.

'There you are.' Guy's quiet voice seemed to echo in the silence, and she jerked round. He was watching her from the edge of the creek, sitting easily on a chestnut horse that tossed its head up and down against the flies, his hat tilted low over his eyes.

He looked solid, overwhelmingly distinct as he sat outlined against the harsh cobalt-blue of the sky. Olivia felt the breath leak slowly out of her. His eyes were shaded by his hat, but the lower half of his face was very clear in the sunlight, the uncompromising jaw, the cool, firm mouth with the creases on either side that deepened to what was almost, but not quite, a smile.

'You shouldn't be out without a hat.' He guided the horse down the bank towards her. 'I saw you heading off into the distance, so I brought you this. Here.' He unhooked a cattleman's hat from the saddle and tossed it down to Olivia, who caught it, much to her surprise, as she edged away from the horse. It looked enormous close up.

The hat was old and stained, the felt torn and battered into shape. She turned it dubiously in her hands. 'I don't know that it's really me,' she said, only half joking.

'As long as it keeps you from getting sunstroke, it doesn't matter whether it's you or not.' Guy's voice was dry. 'That perfect English complexion of yours isn't used to sun like this, and the last thing I need is you sick on my hands. Go on, put it on.'

With a sigh, Olivia obeyed. The hat sat a little askew on her shining hair, framing the pure lines of her face. Beneath the brim, her eyes were wide and very blue.

There was an arrested expression in Guy's eyes as he looked down at her, standing in the dappled shade of the gums. It was hard to believe this was the smart, sophisticated woman in the Townsville hotel, but, if anything, the faded shirt and battered hat served to emphasise her vivid beauty and indefinable glamour. Without taking his eyes from her face, he swung himself effortlessly out of the saddle.

'You look all right in it,' he said, tipping his hat back slightly in an unconscious gesture.

Afflicted by sudden shyness, Olivia stooped to pick up some more gum leaves. 'It's so quiet here,' she said, the first thing she could think of. She concentrated on tearing the leaves between her fingers, trying not to think about how *right* Guy looked in these surroundings.

'It's peaceful.' He glanced around him at the silent, leaning gums silhouetted against the sky, at the sharp contrast between the dazzling light and solid blocks of shade, and the lovely girl standing in front of him in the absurdly battered hat, head bent over her shredding fingers. His horse shifted its legs and blew softly through its nose. 'Don't you think so?'

'I don't know,' Olivia confessed. She scattered the shredded remains on the creek bed and moved away—as if casually, she hoped—from Guy's disturbing solidity. 'I've always lived and worked in cities. I listen to music the whole time, and, even if there's no music, there are always other noises in the background. Here there's nothing. No cars, no sirens, no music, no neighbours arguing. Just . . . silence.'

'You'll get used to it. You might even find you get to like it.'

'You might get used to the cowboy technique, Olivia. You might even find you get to like it.' Guy's words from last night reverberated round the creek in a rush of memory, and for a moment she felt as if he had just kissed her again, her lips tender, her body aroused.

She drew a shaky breath. 'There seem to be an awful lot of things I have to get used to, don't there, Guy?' Her voice was sharper than she had intended, as if in self-defence, and the memory of last night hung between them, a tangible thing.

There was a silence. Guy half turned away and ran his hand over his horse's neck. 'It wasn't just the hat,' he said unexpectedly. 'I followed you because I wanted to apologise for last night.' He hesitated, turned back to look at her again. 'I shouldn't have kissed you like that.'

Olivia moistened her lips. She literally couldn't think of anything to say. 'I . . . I think we were both on edge last night,' she said eventually.

'I thought you'd like to know that it won't happen again.'

'Oh.' Olivia was caught unawares by the sharp, unexpected twist of disappointment. What on earth was the matter with her? This was what she wanted, wasn't it? 'Well, I—er—perhaps it would be best. Let's just forget about last night.' Some chance!

'If that's what you want.' Guy's eyes were cool, uncomfortably observant. 'I'd rather keep things as they were, but if you feel you'd prefer a separate room ...?'

Here was her chance. All she had to do was say, Yes, I would. Instead she tucked her hair behind her ears in a nervous gesture. 'No, it's all right. We agreed.' She tried to make a joke of it. 'If I want you to kiss me again, I'll put in a written request in triplicate, at least a week in advance, so there's no misunderstanding!'

'A simple "please" would do.'

The silence in the creek seemed to intensify as Olivia lifted her eyes almost reluctantly to meet Guy's gaze. It was impossible to tell whether he was amused or serious. All she knew was that it was equally impossible to look away. She could only stand and stare and wish she couldn't remember his every touch quite so clearly.

As the silence lengthened, tightened, the air between them began to jangle with inexplicable tension. Olivia could feel it growing, almost as if it were urging her to take a step forward and say that "please", and she fought down the sensation in panic.

She was so on edge that when Guy's horse snorted violently and danced towards her, tossing its head up and down, she gave a gasp of fright and stepped hurriedly backwards, only to stumble over a fallen branch and land unceremoniously on her bottom.

But at least it had broken the tension.

'Can't you keep it under control?' she demanded, torn between fright and humiliation.

Guy lifted an eyebrow as he put out a casual hand to catch the bridle. 'He's only got a fly up his nose,' he said, a trace of amusement in his voice. 'You'd dance around too.'

The horse gave a final snort and stood docile once more, ears flickering as the insects continued to buzz around its head. Olivia viewed it with a hostile eye. 'It practically charged me!' she said sulkily, feeling foolish.

'Don't be silly, Olivia.' Guy reached down and pulled her to her feet.

His touch was impersonal, his fingers strong and cool, but she felt her senses jolt as if at an electric shock. She pulled her arm quickly away to make a great show of dusting herself down, uncomfortably aware of her own erratic pulse and the taut, controlled power of the man beside her.

'I thought you told us you weren't frightened of horses?'

'I'm not,' she lied coldly. 'It just startled me, that's all.'

'Well, go on, stroke his nose, then. He won't bite.'

Olivia hesitated, then remembered her determination to prove to Guy that she was just as good as anyone else in the outback. The horse rolled its eye and shook the flies off its mane. She put out a hand gingerly, barely brushed the animal's nose and whipped her hand back to stand with defiantly folded arms.

Guy shook his head in disbelief. 'Was that supposed to be a stroke?' He rubbed his hand affectionately between the horse's eyes. 'Or is that how *sophisticated* people like you and Tim touch each other?'

The reference to her gibe last night was unfair. Olivia flushed angrily, but her reply was smothered by a gasp of surprise as Guy pulled her suddenly round to stand wedged between his body and the horse. Holding her easily with one arm, with his free hand he took hers and forced her to stroke the horse with slow, gentle movements. He made her feel its soft, velvet mouth, the warm breath on her palm. '*This* is a stroke,' he said, near her ear.

Olivia's pulse was beating in time to the insistent thud of her heart. Everything seemed to be happening in slow motion. His hand covering hers stood out in vivid relief—the broad wrist with its dark hairs, the creases over each knuckle, the faint scar running diagonally down from one finger. She watched, almost hypnotised, as it moved up and down the horse's nose. She was excruciatingly aware of Guy breathing close to her, of the feel of his hand on hers, of the smell of the horse and the bright blocks of light and shadow.

'It's not so difficult, is it?' he asked.

'N-no.' Olivia hated herself for stammering like a shy schoolgirl, resented the way her every sense was vibrating. With an effort she pulled her hand away. 'I'd better get back. It must be almost time for tea.'

Guy's eyes were cool, amused as he watched her. If he thought she was so damned funny, why didn't he smile? she wondered in frustration, certain that he could see her knees shaking. That crease at the side of his mouth had definitely deepened. She wouldn't mind so much if only he would smile, properly, just once, at her...

'Why don't you ride back?' he suggested.

'No!' Olivia said quickly, and then, with an assumption of nonchalance, 'I mean, I'd rather walk.'

'A real Willagong woman would never be out of the saddle,' Guy said, gathering the reins into one hand and swinging himself effortlessly back on to the horse.

She took off the hat and shook back her hair, challenge in her blue-green eyes. 'But I'm not a real Willagong woman, am I?'

He looked down at her for a moment. 'We'll have to see if we can turn you into one, then,' he said quietly. 'And don't let me catch you out without a hat again.' Pulling the horse's head round, he rode along the creek and up the far bank without once looking back.

Olivia stared after him. Part of her wanted to shout that she didn't want to be a Willagong woman, she didn't care what he thought, she couldn't care less that he never smiled. Another part wanted to stand quite still in the bright light and remember how it had felt to be held against him.

Sighing, she kicked up a spray of leaves. Was it too much to expect a man to smile? He smiled at David, he smiled at Joe and Darren, he even smiled at his horse. Why wouldn't he smile at her?

'I'm his wife,' she said out loud to the hat in her hand. 'I've a right to be smiled at!'

# CHAPTER SIX

OLIVIA blew the dust off *The Aerophos Cookbook* and sat back on her heels to flick through the yellowed pages. Apple Brown Betty, Anzac Biscuits, Fruit Cobbler—this was just what she needed! Turning the book over, she glanced at the date. 1958. That would be about right for the culinary tastes around Willagong Creek!

She got to her feet and brushed herself down. Who would have thought she would ever have been pleased to have found such an old-fashioned collection of baking recipes? Or that she would have become such a dedicated housekeeper?

She glanced around the living area with satisfaction. She had worked hard on this room; the wooden floor was scrubbed, the rugs beaten of all the accumulated dust, the furniture polished. Only these shelves, with their tattered, dated books, remained to be thoroughly cleaned and sorted.

Allowing herself a few moments' rest, Olivia sat in one of the armchairs and let the peace of the house settle about her. It could do with a fresh coat of paint, of course, but this really *was* rather a nice room. She was succumbing gradually to the charm of the house, she realised. Her first appalled reaction had turned to determination to see it clean, and now to reluctant affection. She had started noticing little details that had escaped her at first: the elegant lace ironwork decorating the veranda, the solid doors lining the corridors, the impression of quiet coolness even when the heat was at its most intense.

'I must be getting used to it,' she said, with a faint smile. Her fingers fluttered the pages of the cookbook absently. She hated the dirt and the flies, the vast sky and eerie silence still made her uncomfortable, but she was slowly establishing a relationship with David and, now that she had given up her attempts to cook interesting meals, the ringers were even appreciating her cooking. Guy had never told her what he had said, but every night now they turned up with their hair slicked damply back from a shower, looking well scrubbed in their clean shirts. Yes, she was definitely getting used to things.

She wasn't getting used to Guy.

She couldn't get used to the way her heart jolted every time he came into the room. She couldn't get used to the rush of memory every time she found herself watching his mouth or his hands. She couldn't get used to lying next to him at night and listening to his breathing.

He had never touched her again. Every night they lay together like strangers, and every night Olivia remembered his touch and thought about what he had said.

'Not until you ask, Olivia.'

'It won't happen again.'

'A simple "please" would do.'

But in the face of his apparent indifference, Olivia retreated behind a façade of brittle politeness, and swept and scrubbed and cleaned and polished in the hope that she would be too tired to remember what it had felt like to be kissed by him. She longed to forget it, longed for her indifference to match his own, but every time he turned his head, or picked up his hat, something would clench inside her.

No, she wasn't getting used to Guy.

It had been a relief when he had flown off to Townsville three days ago, but as soon as he'd gone, Olivia had found that she missed him. The veranda felt empty without him, the bed, normally so tense and awkward because he was lying so close, was more uncomfortable than ever.

Half ashamed, she encouraged the ringers to talk about Guy. Corky told her he had worked on the Richardson family property for years. 'Guy, he always knew what he was doing, even as a nipper. Course, the Richardsons are a well-known family in these parts and the Pingunaguna property is one of the best. Guy could have stayed there or taken over as manager of one of their properties the other side of Cloncurry, but he's never been one to choose the easy way. Not many people would have been prepared to take on a run-down property like Willagong.' Corky blew out cigarette smoke and contemplated the problem facing Guy with grim satisfaction. 'It's a good feeling to see land like this put back on its feet.'

Olivia looked doubtfully at the ramshackle buildings. 'He doesn't seem to be getting very far.'

'It all takes time, Mrs R. Guy's no fool. He bought the land cheap, and the market's good this year—no thanks to that European Community or whatever it calls itself.' Corky spat over the rail of the cookhouse veranda. 'There's a lot more cattle here than we thought. We're still mustering to count them all. I dunno how Guy knew—I reckon he's just got a nose for it.'

'There's a lot of wild horses out there too,' Joe added. 'We had to muster them in with the cattle.'

'What happens to them?' Olivia asked.

'You can't do nothing with the brumbies,' said Corky, 'but we pick out the best of them and break them in as work horses. You should see Guy break in some of those broncos, Mrs R. They're madder than fire, those horses, and as mean as can be. They'll do anything to get you off their backs, but Guy just sits there, and they're nuzzling him by the time he gets off! It's something to see the way he brings them under control, I can tell you.'

Olivia could imagine the scene vividly—the frantic, bucking horse and the cool, unyielding will of the man. 'How does he do it?'

'You can't explain it, Mrs R. It's in the hands.' Corky shook his head slowly. 'But them horses, they just know it's no use fighting him.'

Corky's words lingered in Olivia's memory, and she thought about Guy as she turned back to the books. 'Them horses, they just know it's no use fighting him.'

Suddenly she stiffened. Overhead was the unmistakable buzz of the plane. He was back! Stifling the urge to run out and wave, she crouched resolutely down by the shelves again. It wouldn't do for Guy to think she had been missing him.

When the ute drew up outside the homestead, she was still wiping mechanically at the books, every nerve alert to his arrival. She could hear the door of the vehicle slam, David's excited voice, the sound of footsteps on the wooden veranda. And then he was there, in the doorway.

Olivia stood up slowly, still clutching the cloth. She felt as if every emotion drained out of her and then came swooshing back with a surge of feeling that left her exhilarated, almost frightened by the way her body had twanged into awareness. It was almost as if she had never seen him properly before. The definite features, the long, cool mouth, the exciting lines of cheek and jaw, the lean, quiet strength, all hit her with devastating effect.

'Hello,' she said huskily.

Guy had stopped at the sight of her, dusty and begrimed by a pile of books. She was wearing his shirt still, with a pair of black leggings, and she looked tired. The golden hair was pushed carelessly behind her ears and there were smudges of dirt on her cheek, but the long, beautiful eyes were shining.

He looked back at her in silence for a long moment before taking off his hat and moving into the room, but all he said was, 'Still cleaning?' He glanced around him at the transformation from dreary abandonment to gracious tranquillity. 'You've done a good job.'

Olivia bent her head and fiddled with the duster in her hands, unwilling for Guy to see how pleased she was by his laconic praise. Fortunately David interrupted before she had to think of a suitable reply.

'Look what Guy brought me from Townsville!'

She looked up guiltily. She hadn't even noticed David coming into the room with Guy. He was holding out a plastic aeroplane, a miniature version of Guy's. 'The propeller goes round and the doors open,' David went on, anxious for her to appreciate every refinement of his new toy.

He swooped the plane up and down, so obviously delighted with it that Olivia couldn't help smiling. She glanced instinctively at Guy and their eyes met over David's head, such warmth of expression in his that her heart almost stopped.

But he wasn't smiling, and the warmth was for David, not for her.

Olivia's smile faltered at the realisation. She turned her head quickly away.

'I hope you thanked Guy nicely, David?'

'Of course!' said David loftily.

'I brought you a present too, Olivia,' Guy said. 'You'll have to thank me nicely as well. In fact, I brought you two presents.'

'That means you'll have to thank him very nicely,' David pointed out self-righteously.

'Presents? For me?' Olivia stared incredulously at the box Guy held out. Putting down the cloth, she wiped her hands on the shirt and took it hesitantly. 'What is it?'

'Open it and see.'

Inside, wedged into polystyrene, lay a cassette player, with six classical cassettes slotted into the empty spaces. Olivia could only look, disbelieving. She had missed having music more than anything else, and now Guy had brought her this! With some of her favourite composers too. How had he known?

She looked up at Guy. 'I . . . don't know what to say.'

'I remembered you saying that you always listened to music. I wasn't sure what you liked, but I thought with your orchestral background I'd be pretty safe with the classics.'

'Oh, yes!' Olivia took a rather shuddery breath. He had been thinking of her while he was away! It was such a wonderful, unexpected, thoughtful present that she felt stupidly like crying. 'I can't tell you how much it will mean to me to have some music.' He was watching her with his dark eyes and she realised that her thanks sounded woefully inadequate. On an impulse she leant forward and kissed his cheek.

When his arms went round her to pull her tight, Olivia didn't panic. She only laid her cheek against his and thought how safe and secure she felt. 'Thank you,' she whispered.

His hands tightened momentarily against her back, then he put her from him abruptly, as if as disconcerted as she by the sudden intimacy. Olivia flushed slightly and stepped back.

'I brought you something else as well,' Guy said. David, plane in one hand, was absorbed in pushing the buttons on the cassette player with the other.

The package was soft, wrapped in tissue paper. Olivia opened it with unsteady hands, catching her breath as she pulled out an ivory silk nightdress that slithered luxuriously between her hands. It was very simple, almost demure, she noticed, instinctively holding the delicate material against her cheek to feel its cool softness. Her eyes met Guy's wordlessly.

'Sick of you tossing and turning at night because you're too hot in that cotton thing,' he said gruffly.

A slow flush started deep inside her and spread inexorably until she felt that every inch of her skin burned red. She had a vivid image of Guy picking out the nightdress for her, of him imagining her wearing it, of his strong brown hands lingering on the silk. 'Guy, I ...' She felt confused, uncertain. Both the cassette player and the nightdress showed that he had thought about her, had noticed far more than she had realised, but his dark eyes gave nothing away, and he was as remote and self-contained as ever. In the end she said only, again, 'Thank you,' but this time she made no move to kiss him.

'I picked up the mail while I was in town.' Guy broke a silence that was suddenly uneasy. 'There are a couple of letters for you.'

Olivia put down the nightdress and took the letters he handed to her. She had written to friends in London to let them know where she was, but this was the first post she had had. She ought to have been thrilled to get some news from home, but her mind was taken up with Guy and the gifts he had brought her.

Forcing herself to show an interest, she turned the letters over. 'Oh, this is from Annie,' she said to fill the silence. 'And this one's from——' She stopped at the sight of familiar writing.

'From who?' Guy was watching her closely.

'It's from Tim,' Olivia said slowly. He was the last person she had expected to write to her.

Guy's face closed. 'You'll want to be on your own when you read that one,' he said. Turning abruptly on his heel, he went out.

Annie's letter was full of gossip, but it all seemed impossibly remote to Olivia, puzzling over Guy's sudden change of mood. Tim had written to congratulate her on her marriage. It was a nice gesture, she thought, folding the letter and putting it back in the envelope. She wondered a little at her own lack of reaction. Had she ever seriously wanted to marry him? It seemed hard to believe now.

She spent the rest of the day speculating about Guy's presents. Slotting a cassette into the player, she finished the bookshelves to the sound of one of Mozart's concertos, but even the music filling the room wasn't enough to take her mind from the silk nightdress and how it would feel to wear it lying next to Guy that night.

When the time came, Olivia was curiously reluctant to put it on. She left Guy sitting on the veranda, and stood at the bedroom window, pulling the silk through her hands. The T-shirt she had been wearing in bed was hot and uncomfortable, but it was safe. The silk nightdress was soft and seductive, and not safe at all.

It whispered over her skin as she slipped it on, and she smoothed the material nervously over her flat stomach. The silk was cool and luxurious, and cut beautifully to emphasise her slenderness, falling to her ankles in one long, fluid line. Olivia kept thinking of Guy holding the nightdress in his hands, the hands that could bring a wild horse under control, and she felt her spine shiver. She was agonisingly aware of her own body, of her nipples stiff and aroused beneath the silk.

Desperate to distract her mind, she crossed to the chest of drawers, the silk swishing against her legs, and picked up her letters. Think about London, think about friends, think about anything except Guy's hands against silk against her skin.

She sat on the edge of the bed and tried to concentrate on Tim's letter, but the words danced before her eyes, and she was staring mindlessly at the paper when the door opened and Guy came in.

Olivia started at his sudden appearance, and dropped the letter. The light airmail paper drifted lazily to the floor to land at Guy's feet. He bent to pick it up.

'Re-reading your love-letter?' he asked harshly.

'It's not a love-letter.' Olivia slid into bed and pulled the sheet over her. Ivory silk was an inadequate protection with his eyes upon her, and she felt more confident with the cotton sheet tugged up to her neck.

Guy seemed angry. 'What did he want, then?'

'Who?'

'Tim. That's who it's from, isn't it? The sophisticated lover you miss so much.'

Safe behind her sheet, Olivia stiffened at the contempt in his voice, and her eyes flashed in challenge. It would have been easy to have simply explained Tim's letter, but she saw no reason to while Guy was being so aggressive. 'I don't have to tell you what's in my private correspondence!' she snapped, and held out her hand. 'I'd like it back, please.'

'Come and get it.' Guy held the letter up and shook it enticingly. 'If it matters that much to you, stop hiding behind that sheet and come and get it!'

Olivia bit her lip. She didn't know why Guy was so suddenly hostile. The shimmer of silk against her body seemed somehow more provocative, more disturbingly erotic than if she had been wearing nothing at all.

Slowly she threw back the sheet and stood up. The silk slithered over her thighs and swung to the floor. Across the room, her eyes met Guy's. He hadn't moved. He just stood there, holding the letter, and watching her, and unconsciously Olivia moistened her lips with her tongue.

'Well, are you coming or not?'

She walked towards him. His jaw was set, his lips pressed together in a firm line, but his eyes seemed to burn with suppressed emotion as they moved over her, from the seductive hollows between throat and clavicle, the honey-warm skin of her shoulders, down to the taut swell of breasts and on, over slenderness, sliding from stomach to the long, slim, ivory silk line of her legs. Olivia felt her skin afire with awareness; where his eyes moved, the silk seemed to burn and caress her skin, sliding against her in tingling intimacy.

She stopped. Her heart was thumping, her mouth dry. Guy was less than an arm's reach away. She could see the clench of his jaw, the muscles working in his throat.

'Can I have my letter?' she managed in a cracked voice, unable to bear the tension any longer.

His eyes seemed to focus abruptly on her face, then dropped to the letter in his hand as if he had forgotten all about it. Very deliberately, he folded it up and, reaching out, tucked it into the shadowy valley between her breasts. His fingers just brushed against her skin, and she drew a sharp breath, half in dread, half in anticipation.

'Here, have it, if that's what you want so much!' he said in a tight voice. Wheeling round, he went out, banging the door behind him and leaving Olivia standing in the middle of the floor, her eyes filled with tears.

He came back later, but no mention was made of the letter or the nightdress. He simply climbed in beside her and settled himself for sleep. That was the pattern for the weeks that followed. Olivia might as well have been another pillow in the bed for all the notice Guy took of her at night.

By day, things were easier, and life fell gradually into a routine. Most afternoons, she would walk with David along the creek. She told him stories, and sometimes they would talk about Diane. David never said much, but she would feel his small body lean wordlessly against hers, as much comforting as comforted.

Succumbing at last to the combined pressure of Guy, David and the ringers, Olivia allowed herself to be persuaded on to a horse, where she clung with grim determination to the saddle while Guy rode slowly beside her. She refused to do more than walk. David soon got bored and cantered ahead, but Guy was unhurried, unperturbed by their leisurely progress.

Olivia wished she looked that at home on a horse. Guy rode through the dry bush as if he were part of it. He pointed out things to her that she would never have noticed, and little by little she learnt about the land and the cattle.

The cassettes he had given her filled the house with music as she cooked and cleaned, and occasionally she caught herself humming along. If it hadn't been for the nights when she had to lie, restless in silken awareness, next to an unresponsive Guy, she might have thought that she was ... well, almost *happy*.

Olivia never forgot the day of the muster. She was up at half-past four to cook breakfast for the men, who were bringing all the cattle from one of the huge paddocks north of the homestead back to the stockyards. There the calves would be separated from their mothers and then branded, castrated and dehorned. Joe, in a rare burst of loquaciousness, had explained the whole process to her in gory detail the night before.

David was in a fever of impatience all day, waiting for the muster to reach the stockyards, and even more importantly to see the helicopter which was going to spot stray cattle from the herd and drive them towards the herd. Guy had told David that Robin, the pilot, would fly straight to Kalunga early in the morning, and wouldn't get to the homestead until the muster did, about five, which meant that David drove Olivia mad by demanding to know the time every few minutes.

She was rolling out pastry for an apple pie when he came pell-mell up the cookhouse steps. 'They're coming! They're coming!'

Wiping her hands on her apron, she followed him out to the stockyards. A cloud of dust on the horizon was moving steadily towards them, and she watched in awe as the pounding hoofs rumbled and vibrated along the ground like far-off thunder. 'How many cattle have they *got* out there?' she asked nervously.

'Lots,' said David.

One moment they were standing alone in the still heat, the next the air was full of bellowing and choking red dust and cracking whips and the piercing *yip-yip* cries of the men on horseback as the cattle surged past into the stockyards in an unstoppable mob.

Alarmed by the noise and rush, Olivia drew David back slightly and placed restraining hands on his shoulders. He was tense with excitement, his eyes shining.

She coughed and blinked through the swirling dust at the scene. Most of the cattle seemed to be inside the sturdy wooden rails by now. They milled around with aggrieved bellows, and, as the dust settled slowly, individual figures emerged. There was Ben, leaning forward on his horse to close the last gate, there were Darren and Joe swinging out of the saddle, and Guy——

As she caught sight of him through the confusion, Olivia's heart missed a beat and then did a jolting kick-start into hammering life again. She wished it wouldn't do that. Guy was sitting on the huge chestnut horse, hat tilted slightly forwards, lasso looped casually round the pommel of his saddle. He was shouting orders to Ben over the noise and holding the horse easily with one hand as it snorted and sidled away from the milling cattle.

It was only a man on a horse. There was absolutely no reason for her heart to start jumping around like that, Olivia told herself crossly. No reason for him to have noticed her through the dust as she had noticed him.

'I'm going back to the kitchen, David,' she said abruptly. 'Don't get under their feet.'

'He can come with me if he likes, Mrs R,' said Corky, materialising beside her. 'I'm going to pick up Robin.'

'Robin?' Olivia repeated, preoccupied with her own thoughts.

'From the chopper.' Corky jerked his head in the direction of the airstrip. 'Saw it land a few minutes ago. You wouldn't have heard it, with all the noise here.'

'Oh, yes, of course.' Olivia glanced down at David with a smile. 'You've been dying to see the helicopter, haven't you, David?'

David nodded, eyes shining with anticipation, and trotted off beside Corky, while Olivia made her way back to the cookhouse and told herself that she didn't care in the least that Guy hadn't looked over and acknowledged her presence with a smile...

Covering the apples with pastry, she knocked up the edges and cut some 'leaves' for decoration. Always an odd number—it was one of the few things she remembered from her cordon bleu course. She admired the pie as she put it in the fridge to rest. Really, she was getting quite good at this kind of thing—apple pies, housework, riding; perhaps she'd make an outback woman yet.

She was chopping parsley when Guy came in. At her request, he had brought her parsley pots back from Townsville. She had planted them in the shade of the cookhouse and nurtured them tenderly. If she was going to have to cook good, plain food, it would at least look nice. The ringers had got used to their evening meal prepared with subtle garnishes. It had become a challenge to Olivia, to see how beautiful she could make something look before eyebrows were raised and doubtful looks exchanged.

Guy looked hot and tired and dusty as he brushed off his hat in a characteristic gesture. 'It's been a long day,' he said.

The urge to go to him and touch him and smooth the tired lines from his face was suddenly so strong that Olivia had to bend her shining head over the chopping board and clench the knife tightly in her hand. 'Would you like a beer?' she asked, sounding stiff and formal.

'I'll get it.' Guy tossed his hat on top of the fridge, opened the door and pulled out a frosty can. He propped himself on a stool opposite her. 'You want to be careful you don't cut yourself with that knife,' he warned. 'It's specially sharpened for butchering.'

'That's precisely why I'm using it!' Olivia said sharply. It was easier to be irritable than to think about touching him. 'It's hopeless trying to chop herbs with a blunt knife. You don't have to be born and bred in the outback to know how to handle a knife. I know perfectly well what I'm doing.'

'Could have fooled me, they way you're waving that one around.' Guy broke off as the ute rattled to a halt outside and doors banged. 'This'll be Robin.'

Expecting another lanky, laconic stockman, Olivia carried on chopping until the screen door opened to admit a petite girl, about five years younger than herself, dressed in the ubiquitous lightly checked shirt, jeans and boots. She had short, softly curling brown hair and a fresh, pretty face. Olivia, who had expended much thought trying to make herself look practical in black leggings and a baggy peacock blue shirt, immediately felt gaudy and out of place.

She laid down the knife and looked enquiringly at the girl, puzzled by her unexpected arrival, and then at Guy. He didn't look surprised. He was smiling at the girl, and Olivia's eyes narrowed fractionally.

David followed close on the girl's heels and looked up worshipfully. 'This is Robin,' he announced.

Olivia's mouth dropped open. '*Robin?* But I thought Robin was a pilot!'

'I am.' The other girl's smile flickered over to Guy with a hint of complacency. 'I suppose you were expecting a man. I'm Robyn with a "y". Didn't Guy tell you?'

# CHAPTER SEVEN

'No,' SAID Olivia coldly.

'Have a beer,' said Guy to Robyn, handing her a can. 'You've earned it.'

'Thanks.' Robyn sent him a sparkling glance of complicity. 'I've been waiting for this ever since you promised it to me this morning!'

Olivia savagely resumed her chopping. It was revolting, the way she was simpering up at him, and as for Guy! She hadn't known he could look so fatuous!

'Robyn showed me her helicopter and I sat at the controls!' David was obviously as besotted as Guy, and Olivia suppressed a twist of hurt that Robyn had won him over so easily when it had taken her weeks to break through his shell. 'She's going to give me a ride in it tomorrow!'

'If that's OK with you, Olivia?' Robyn added.

'Of course.' Olivia mustered a smile. 'As long as it's safe.'

'Safe as houses—Guy and I spent most of the morning in it!'

'Really?' Olivia said frostily, and glanced at Guy, who was leaning against the fridge and watching them both with his usual unreadable expression.

Very much at home, Robyn perched herself on the table and swung her legs, but in spite of her little-girl posture her brown eyes were cool as she raised her can to Olivia. 'Anyway, congratulations.'

'Congratulations?' Olivia looked blank.

'On your marriage,' Robyn explained, with a speculative look. 'We'd all given up hope of Guy ever getting married.' She was obviously wondering why on earth he had picked such a patently unsuitable wife. 'You hadn't known each other very long, had you?'

'No.' Olivia was quick to pick up the suspicious note in the other girl's voice, and she looked uneasily at Guy. He met her look blandly, and she lifted her chin as she turned back to Robyn. Was she the girlfriend David had mentioned? 'How long have you known Guy?' she asked stiffly.

'Oh, forever! I grew up on the neighbouring property. We're practically family! I flew Guy round Willagong Creek when he first bought it— do you remember, Guy? It looks a bit different now!'

'You'll see a difference in the homestead too,' Guy told her. 'Olivia's cleaned it all out.'

'I always rather liked it the way it was,' Robyn said prettily. 'Still, you're lucky to have found yourself such an efficient housekeeper. I'm awful,' she turned to Olivia with a confiding air, 'I hate being stuck in a house. That's why I learned to fly; it gets me outside with the men.'

'You're obviously one of the lads,' Olivia said with a tight smile, hating Robyn, who was accepted by the men, who wasn't prepared to do the dreary woman's work that she clearly thought was all Olivia was fit for.

'I've always been a tomboy,' Robyn sighed with mock regret. 'I don't mind cooking if I have to—in fact, my Anzac biscuits are famous, aren't they, Guy?' Without waiting for his answer, she went on, 'I took some with me for smoko. The boys love them.' She paused. 'Your rock cakes were good too, of course, Olivia.'

Of course, Robyn with a "y" *would* have taken something for smoko! Olivia, who knew quite well that her rock cakes had been disastrously hard and burnt—she had tried to make them several times for Joe, who claimed they were his favourites, but the secret had so far eluded her—tightened her hands round her knife and carried on chopping.

'David,' Guy intervened quietly, 'why don't you show Robyn over to the homestead when she's finished her beer?'

'Oh, I know my way!' Robyn drained her beer and jumped off the table. 'Where shall I put my stuff? In my usual room?'

'I made up the bed next to David's,' Olivia said in a glacial voice. 'I don't know if that's your usual room or not.'

There was silence in the cookhouse as David trotted off beside Robyn, chattering about helicopters.

'Why didn't you tell me Robyn was a woman?' Olivia asked at last, accusingly.

Guy sat back on his stool. 'I didn't think about it,' he said.

'Oh, really?' Olivia slammed down the knife and went to put the apple pie in the oven. 'Funny thing not to think about when you're *such* good friends!'

Guy was unresponsive to her sarcasm. 'I've known Robyn since she was a kid,' he said calmly, 'and she's been a lot of help to me since I bought this property. She's a real outback girl; she understands how things work out here.'

'Unlike me, I suppose!'

'Unlike you,' he agreed equably.

Olivia scraped the parsley into a bowl and began to peel some onions. 'I don't suppose her *usual room* could be the one I'm sleeping in, could it? I'd hate to think I was keeping such soulmates apart! Sure you wouldn't like me to move out and let her take my place?'

She put the knife down nervously as Guy placed both hands flat on the table and leant forward so that his eyes were boring into hers. 'Bed-hopping may be par for the course where you come from, but it's not out here. You're my wife, Olivia, not Robyn, and that means you sleep with me.' He straightened. 'You're giving a fine impression of a jealous wife. You don't need to pretend when it's just me, you know.'

'Jealous?' Olivia shook back her hair angrily and picked up another onion. 'I'm not jealous. I couldn't care less what you get up to together in her precious helicopter!'

Guy sat back on his stool. The almost-smile was lurking about his mouth. 'I hate to spoil your image of me, but it would take a better man than me to make love to a woman in a helicopter just a few feet above the ground, chasing cattle and avoiding trees at the same time.' He paused and looked at Olivia, her face stormy above the vivid blue of her shirt. 'Depends on the woman, of course.'

'I'm sure Robyn could manage it,' Olivia said waspishly. 'Being such an *outback girl*!'

'As you're my wife, I expect you to be pleasant to Robyn.' Guy's voice was quiet but implacable. 'Not only is she a friend, she's an essential part of the team. I need a helicopter on these musters. I haven't got enough men or enough time otherwise, so you're going to have to get used to her being around a lot over the next few weeks. While she's here, I don't want you putting on airs and graces and intimidating her.'

'Me? Intimidate Robyn?' Olivia stared incredulously at Guy, then yelped as the butchering knife slipped across the smooth surface of the onion and sliced into her knuckle. 'Ouch!' The blood welled to the surface and she sucked frantically at the cut.

'I told you to be careful with that knife!' Guy was round the table before she realised he had moved. He dragged her unceremoniously over to the sink and held her hand under the cold tap. 'It serves you right!'

'Thanks for the sympathy!' Olivia tugged her hand away to inspect the wound. It was a tiny cut, but very deep, and the bone gleamed whitely through the blood.

'You don't deserve any sympathy after the way you were waving that knife around,' Guy said crossly, then broke off to peer at her. 'Olivia? Are you all right?'

There was a loud roaring in her ears. 'I'm fine,' said Olivia, and keeled forward gracefully.

Guy caught her before she hit the floor. Muttering under his breath, he lifted the slim body in his arms and deposited her ungently in a chair, pushing her head between her knees.

She came to to the feel of Guy's hand, reassuringly capable on the nape of her neck. 'What happened?' she asked weakly.

'You fainted at the sight of that ghastly wound.' His voice was dry. He rummaged in one of the cupboards for a plaster and stuck it over her knuckle with brisk efficiency. 'Can you walk?'

Furious with herself for giving him yet another opportunity to write her off as a squeamish 'city girl', Olivia stood up abruptly. 'Of course I can walk!' But her legs buckled as a wave of nausea swept over her, and she clutched at the nearest thing, which happened to be Guy's arm.

'I think you'd better lie down for a bit.' She couldn't decide whether he sounded exasperated or amused as he lifted her easily into his arms again.

'I don't need to lie down. I feel fine.' She felt awful, distinctly queasy and fuzzy, as if she were made of cotton wool.

Guy ignored her, and carried her down the steps and across to the homestead. The feel of his arms about her was inexpressibly comforting, and Olivia suddenly longed to give in and lean her head against his shoulder. Her face could rest just under his jaw; her lips would be a mere breath away from his throat. He smelt of dust and sun and horses.

She was just about to relax in his arms when Robyn's clear voice called out from the veranda, 'What's the matter with Olivia?'

Olivia stiffened. 'Put me down!' she muttered to Guy, who gave no sign of having heard her.

'She'll be all right. She just fainted,' he said to Robyn as he climbed the veranda steps with his burden.

'Fainted? Why?'

What business was it of hers? Olivia thought with a scowl. 'I cut myself,' she said sulkily. 'There's nothing wrong with me.'

Robyn was looking fresh and neat in clean jeans and pale blue chambray shirt, her curls still damp from the shower. Like Guy, she looked utterly right in her surroundings, and Olivia, who knew that, no matter how hard she tried, she would never look as if she belonged, felt a wave of depression wash over her.

'Well, let me know if you want me to take over in the kitchen.'

There was no doubt that Robyn would be able to take over everything, Olivia thought bleakly. She wouldn't shriek at David's insects. She wouldn't faint at the first sight of blood. She would be able to cook the men the sort of meal they liked, plain and ungarnished, and she wouldn't alarm them by appearing in a dress. She would look at home and talk to them about things they knew, and they would all wish it was Robyn Guy had married instead of that peculiar Pom.

A dull sense of her own inadequacy settled inside her like a stone. She had been fooling herself when she had thought she was adjusting. She could never be like Robyn, never be the suitable sort of girl that Guy would really want to marry.

'Are you all right?' Guy asked, as he laid her on the bed.

'I'm fine,' Olivia said listlessly, and turned her head away. Her hand ached, her head ached, her heart ached, and she didn't want to think about how bereft she felt without Guy's arms around her.

There was an unsettling intimacy in watching him move about the room, stripping off his watch, unbuckling his belt, unbuttoning his shirt. Olivia saw him with a strange new clarity, as if for the first time, every detail about him clear and distinct. She had always made a point of leaving the room, or pretending to be asleep, when Guy dressed or undressed. Now she couldn't take her eyes off him.

Her gaze rested on the long, clean line of his back, the powerful shoulders and firm, tanned skin as he stripped off his shirt and sat down on the other side of the bed to pull off his boots.

'You'd better stay here for a bit,' he said over his shoulder. 'I've never seen anyone faint from such a small cut before.'

For once Olivia didn't respond. He stood up and stretched, rippling the muscles in his shoulders, and her stomach clenched with the impossible need to reach out and touch him.

Unhurried, assured, Guy walked across the room with his peculiarly controlled grace, and pulled a towel from the back of a chair. Suddenly Olivia wanted desperately for him to turn and smile at her. Really smile. She wanted him to turn and open his arms so that she could slip her own about him and feel his skin beneath her hands. She wanted to rest her cheek against his chest and listen to his heart beating. She wanted him to hold her close and kiss her the way he had done before. She wanted him to want her the way she desperately, desperately wanted him.

'Are you sure you're all right, Olivia?' He was watching her from the end of the bed. The towel was slung round his neck, and one eyebrow was raised at her expression of appalled realisation.

'What?' Olivia, jerked back to awful reality, could only stare at him with wide, troubled blue eyes.

'You look very strange.' Guy looked at her thoughtfully. 'Is something the matter?'

*Yes.* 'N-no, of course not!' Horrified to find herself stammering, Olivia slid her eyes away from that searching gaze.

Guy stood looking down at her in silence, his expression half irritated, half concerned, then he shrugged. 'In that case, I'll go and wash.'

As the door closed behind him, Olivia sank back on to the pillows and stared unseeingly at the ceiling. How had it happened? And why had it taken her until now to realise the truth?

She was in love with her husband.

The meal that night was a disaster. By the time Olivia got back to the kitchen the apple pie was burnt and the vegetables overcooked. Still overwhelmed by new emotions, she put sugar in the gravy instead of salt, then stood clutching the wooden spoon while the gravy congealed unnoticed in the roasting dish.

Robyn was clearly unimpressed, and her glances at Guy were sympathetic. Olivia was too miserable to care. Why on earth had she allowed this to happen? It had been just another business deal; at the end of it all she was going to walk back into her sophisticated life. How could she have fallen in love with Guy, of all people? He wasn't handsome, he wasn't charming, he certainly wasn't in love with *her*. He just sat at the end of the table and *looked* like that, and she felt her bones melt with wanting him.

Perfectly at home, Robyn laughed and chatted to the men. Everything about her seemed designed to point out how alien and unsuitable Olivia was. Olivia's pride rebelled at last, and she retreated behind a barrier of frigid sophistication, but if Guy noticed how brittle and aloof she appeared he made no comment.

The next morning was even worse. After a sleepless night next to Guy, who ignored her throughout, Olivia was tense and unhappy, and determined not to show it. She struggled through breakfast and then, to prove how relaxed and comfortable she felt, strolled down to the stockyards where the calves were being forced through a grisly routine. Separated from their mothers, they were wrestled into clamps. A burning brand was seared into their rumps and their horns were clipped off with what looked to Olivia like barbaric cruelty. Shaking their heads, dazed with shock, blood spouting in a bright red gush from what remained of their horns, the animals were released into a holding yard where they milled around, bellowing in protest.

Appalled at the smell and the blood and the rough handling, Olivia watched for about a minute before fleeing back to the kitchen. Her hands shook as she washed them at the sink, sickened by what she had seen and ashamed by her own squeamishness. She would never, ever belong here! David had been hanging over the rails, watching with interest, Robyn had been branding, working side by side with Guy, with calm, capable hands, their faces absorbed. And she, Olivia, couldn't even watch! Guy must be embarrassed to have such a wife!

Robyn was so clearly suitable that she wondered why Guy hadn't married her long ago.

Drearily, she made her way over to the cold store. There was still lunch to prepare, meals to be cooked, another day to be got through. As she reached blindly into a sack for some onions, her hand brushed over something that moved sickeningly in response, and she leapt back, pulling over the sack. Onions tumbled out around her feet, and through them slithered a small brown snake.

Olivia didn't stop to think. Clapping her hands to her ears, she screamed. The snake, disturbed from its coiled sleep, writhed quickly back into the dark behind the sacks lining the walls. Olivia shuddered with disgust and began to back away in the opposite direction towards the door, as if the snake had retired merely to plan another attack. The relief as her hand touched the screen door was indescribable, and she stumbled down the steps in time to see Guy running over from the yards.

'What is it?' he demanded, grabbing her by the shoulders. 'Why were you screaming?'

Olivia, shaken, humiliated, exhausted from lack of sleep, burst into tears.

'This bloody place! I hate it! I hate it!'

Guy's brows snapped together. 'What's the matter?'

'There was a snake! In the onion sack.' She gulped back another sob. 'I touched it!'

'Did it bite you? Are you hurt?' His hands tightened against her shoulders.

'N-no.'

Guy relaxed slightly. 'You——'

'Oh, don't tell me!' Olivia interrupted him, crying uncontrollably now with the pent-up feelings of the past few weeks. 'I'll get used to it—that's what you were going to say, wasn't it? Well, I won't! I'll never get used to it!' Wrenching herself from his grasp, she ran sobbing towards the creek.

'Olivia!' Guy called, but she ignored him, half blinded by tears as she blundered down the bank and into the drifts of fragrant gum leaves. The trees leant over her, shading her from the harsh sky and cocooning her in quiet.

'Olivia.' Guy caught up with her easily. 'What's the matter with you?'

'Willagong Creek's the matter with me!' she shouted back at him hysterically, heedless of the tears streaming down her face. 'I hate it here! I hate the flies and I hate the dirt and I hate the fact that every time I open a drawer or put my hand in a sack there's some horrible creature waiting to jump out at me! You think all I'm good for is cooking and cleaning, and I can't even do that very well, and I didn't want to ride, but you made me, and I *hate* horses, and you all hate me because I can't brand a c-cow!' She trailed off into helpless, hiccuping sobs.

There was a hateful suspicion of a smile in Guy's voice. 'We don't hate you, Olivia.'

'Yes, you do! I can't do any of the things you want me to do. You didn't want me to stay, and you were right! Well, I've had enough! You can keep your precious outback—I want to go home!'

She turned away and for a long moment there was only the sound of her jerky crying in the still creek.

'What about David?' Guy said quietly.

'He doesn't need me! He'd much rather b-be with Robyn.'

'No, he wouldn't.' Guy turned her firmly back to face him. 'He'd miss you more than you know; more than he knows, probably.'

When she only shook her head miserably, the tangled golden hair swinging in front of her face, he pulled her close against him. 'He would,' he insisted. His hands were warm and strong against her back, moving gently, as if he were soothing a quivering animal.

Olivia took a juddering breath and leant against him. The feel of his arms about her was infinitely reassuring. Slowly the hysterical, frustrated anger subsided, and it was enough to rest her face against his neck and feel him breathing.

'I'm sorry,' she muttered at last. 'I don't know what came over me.'

'Do you really want to go home?' Guy asked above her head, and she could feel his chest vibrating as he spoke.

'No,' she whispered. She knew she ought to pull herself together, move away, show him that she was all right, but it just felt so comfortable being held by him. 'I was just being . . . stupid. I didn't mean all I said. I don't want to leave David.' I don't want to leave you. The words trembled on her lips, but something held her back. Guy had only mentioned David, hadn't he?

'I know it's been difficult for you,' he said surprisingly. 'If you did want to go... if you ever find that you really can't cope——'

'I *can* cope!' she said into his neck, rather muffled, wanting to pull away, to look confident, wanting more to kiss the pulse beating below his ear. Her lips were almost touching it, *almost* ...

His mouth was close to her silken hair. 'Good girl,' was all he said.

There was no reason for them not to step apart. Olivia even expected him to put her firmly away from him, but he didn't. Neither moved, but something indefinable changed. The comfort, the reassurance seeped away and a deeper, more exciting feeling took their place. Guy's hands continued to smooth rhythmically up and down her back; perhaps his arms tightened imperceptibly, perhaps Olivia pressed just that tiny bit closer. Her breath shortened as a quivering deep inside her erupted without warning into a burning awareness of their bodies touching, holding each other, of Guy's warmth and strength and the aching need to lift her face so that he could kiss her...

'Guy! Is everything OK?' Guy's hands stilled suddenly, as Robyn's voice called from the creek bank. 'Oh, sorry!' The other girl had obviously just caught sight of the two of them standing so close together. 'You've been gone so long,' she excused herself. 'We wondered what was happening.'

Guy released Olivia slowly, almost reluctantly. 'It's all right,' he said up to Robyn. 'I'm just coming.'

It was a clear dismissal. Robyn hesitated, then walked away, leaving Guy looking down at Olivia. '*Are* you all right?'

'Yes.' Olivia's eyes skittered away to the trees. 'Yes, I'm OK.'

'I'd better get back, then.'

'Yes.' What could she say? Don't leave me? Don't go? Stay here and kiss me? Lay me down on the scented leaves and make love to me?

With a final look, Guy turned and began to walk after Robyn. 'Guy?' Olivia called, suddenly desperate.

'Yes?'

'I...I *am* sorry.' She lifted her head, her eyes deep and blue. 'I won't make a scene like that again.'

'Will you be coming along later, or would you like me to take the smoko with me?' Robyn asked from her vantage point on a big, snorting horse. The men had just started moving the cattle back out to a new area, and the dust was slowly settling back into place in the now strangely silent stockyards as they receded into the distance.

'I'll bring it,' Olivia said firmly, edging away from the horse.

'We'll stop at Kinvalier—oh, I'd better take something now, after all. You can't get a vehicle up there, and you don't ride, do you?'

Olivia bristled, and her turquoise eyes flashed. 'Who told you that?'

'I know you go out with Guy and David sometimes, but this would be a long ride on your own.'

'I'm perfectly capable of riding out to Kinvalier!' Olivia snapped.

Robyn looked unconvinced. 'There's no need for you to come, you know. Guy wouldn't mind if you stayed.'

Oh, wouldn't he? 'Tell Guy,' said Olivia through gritted teeth, 'that *I* will be bringing the smoko. I'll be with you about half-past ten.'

Later, eyeing her horse's flattened ears, she wondered what on earth had possessed her to make such a stupid boast. She wasn't at all sure she could even saddle the horse, let alone ride all the way out to Kinvalier. Why, oh, why hadn't she just handed over the fruit scones and stayed quietly at home?

'Because you don't want Robyn to be alone with Guy,' she reminded herself, forgetting the presence of the four ringers and David, who had been allowed to go as long as he stayed close to Robyn.

When Guy had left her standing in the creek, Olivia had come to a decision. There would be no more tears, no more embarrassing scenes. She was in love with Guy, and she was going to make him love her, no matter what it took. If a Willagong woman was what he wanted, that was what she would have to become.

Willagong woman rode, so she would too. She took a firm grip on the bridle, and advanced towards the horse.

By the time she neared Kinvalier, it was past eleven o'clock and she was exhausted. Sensing the lack of a firmer hand, the horse played up, but she had clung on with grim determination. She had fallen off twice, and had been so enraged by the time she had caught the horse and remounted the second time that she had jerked the reins and kicked her heels into its ribs with a fury that had surmounted every fear. The horse, as if recognising a stronger will, had behaved beautifully since, but now, as they came in sight of the herd, it pricked up its ears and increased its pace, as if catching some of the excitement.

Scarlet with effort, Olivia hauled on the reins, but to no avail, and to her horror the horse broke into an alarming gallop. She clung desperately to the saddle, coughing and spluttering at the dust and shouting furious curses at the horse. They had obviously been waiting for her, for the cattle had straggled to a halt with no cracking whips or chivvying horses to keep them going. Now they either grazed or blundered out of the way with big, incurious brown eyes.

Quite out of control now, the horse and its dishevelled rider galloped on towards the small group who were watching their progress with varying expressions of incredulity. Only one figure, sitting easy on his horse, came cantering through the dust to catch Olivia's horse and bring it firmly to a stop.

It was Guy, and he was smiling.

## CHAPTER EIGHT

THEY lit a fire, sheltering the first flickering flame with a hat, and boiled tea in the billy. Olivia cupped her hands around a battered enamel mug and hugged her happiness to her like a secret.

She didn't care that she was hot and sweaty and sore. It didn't matter that she had looked ridiculous, careering out of control, clutching ineffectually at the reins. It didn't even matter that Robyn was there, handling her horse with consummate skill. All she cared about was Guy. He had smiled at her, the heart-shaking smile she had been waiting for, and had led her over to join the others as if he was proud of her.

'Well done,' he had said quietly as he reached her. 'I never thought you'd really ride out on your own. What happened to the girl who was frightened of horses?'

'She fell off!' Olivia said, rubbing herself ruefully where she had hit the ground.

'You did look funny!' David giggled. 'You were bouncing around all over the place. We thought you were going to come off, but you didn't.'

'Yeah, we'll make a rider of her yet, eh?' Ben teased. 'We'll have you bareback in no time, Mrs R.'

134

'Perhaps we could put her into the rodeo tomorrow?' suggested Darren, entering into the spirit of things. 'What about the bucking bronco?'

'I feel as if I've already done that!' Olivia said with a meaningful look at her horse, who was standing placidly nearby, the picture of innocence.

'I didn't know that old horse could move that fast,' said Corky, poking at the fire with a twig. 'I've never seen it move at more than a trot before.'

'The beastly thing is completely wild,' Olivia declared, but for once she didn't feel excluded by their laughter and grinned back.

It felt good to be out there with them, hunkered down beside the fire. The ringers bantered amongst themselves, and teased Olivia unmercifully about her riding ability, although she sensed that they admired her for having overcome her fear.

Robyn clearly couldn't imagine why they were making so much fuss over her. 'I'd no idea it was going to be quite such a performance for you, Olivia,' she said condescendingly. 'You should have let me bring the smoko as I suggested.'

'The important thing is that she did it,' Guy put in before Olivia could reply. 'Now she knows she can ride if she has to.' He glanced back at Olivia. She was sitting looking down at the fire as she cradled the mug in her hands. 'You might even get to like it, Olivia.'

'You might even find you get to like it.' That phrase again, echoing with memories of the last time he had kissed her. Did he remember? The battered old hat he had given her shaded her face until she looked up and met his eyes across the fire, her own an intense blue.

'I might,' she said.

The thought of getting back into the saddle was unappealing, but they ignored her protests, pulling her stiffly to her feet and throwing her up on to the horse. David was delegated to ride back to the homestead with her, and Olivia was touched at the way he agreed, disappointment at missing the rest of the day warring with the manful way he shouldered responsibility for the poor, helpless woman. Looking up, she saw Guy watching them with evident amusement, and she smiled over David's head as she caught his eye. Guy smiled slowly back, and giddy, dizzy exhilaration washed through her.

Olivia wafted home, bruised muscles forgotten. She responded absently to David's chatter, dreaming of Guy's smile. It was only a movement of facial muscles, merely a display of teeth. What was it about it that lit up the world, making even this sun-baked country brighter, clearer, as if everything had been thrown into sharper focus?

The smile stayed with her all day as she cleaned the kitchen and prepared a meal for when the men returned. It took her ages to sweep the veranda, as she kept drifting off into a dream world where Guy would smile at her again. He would take her in his arms, pull her towards him with his strong brown hands . . . here Olivia shivered with pure desire and blinked herself back to reality. She was clutching the broom ridiculously against her chest, and although there was no one to see, she flushed as she hurriedly resumed sweeping.

He had only smiled at her! It was hardly a declaration of love, she reminded herself, mindlessly scattering at least five times their normal amount of feed to the chickens, who clucked contentedly about her feet, unable to believe their good luck. It was silly to get so worked up about it.

But reason stood no chance against the fever pumping through her veins. She couldn't think about anything but Guy, about the need to see him smile at her again, to feel him touch her once more.

'Not until you ask.'

The idea settled in her head, impossible to dislodge. Could she ask? Did she dare? What would he say if she did?

When he returned, she was still trying to decide, and she avoided his eyes as much as possible, fearful that she might suddenly blurt it out in front of everyone.

They must have talked over the meal, Olivia supposed, but she couldn't recall any of it. She tried not to look at Guy, but it was hopeless. Her eyes kept crawling over him, as if she could touch him physically, while she twisted and squirmed with a desire so strong that it could be denied no longer.

If he wouldn't touch her until she asked, she would ask. She would have to.

But it wasn't that easy. At last everything was cleared away and goodnights said. At last the generator was switched off, leaving the homestead in uncanny silence. Guy was still talking to Robyn on the veranda as Olivia slipped the silk nightdress over her head and wondered how she would ever find the right words.

She lay between the sheets and practised alternatives. 'Would you...?' 'Could you...?' 'I wondered if...?' Perhaps 'would you mind' would be better? Too stilted. A simple 'please', as Guy had suggested? No, it sounded too abrupt by itself.

Olivia tossed and turned. Where was he? What was he talking to Robyn about all this time? Why didn't he come?

It felt like hours before he came in, closing the door softly behind him. Immediately all Olivia's carefully rehearsed phrases fell away and she lay dumbly as he undressed and slid in beside her.

Now. Go on, say it! But her tongue felt thick and unwieldy in her mouth and she could only stare helplessly into the darkness, trapped in a straitjacket of shyness.

Later, when the deep, even breathing beside her told her Guy was asleep, she slipped noiselessly out of bed and went to stand at the window. The night air was cool and soothing against her hot skin, and she turned her face up to the moonlight. Why hadn't she said anything? Surely they weren't such hard words to say? Would she ever have the courage to try again?

'Can't you sleep?'

Olivia started at the sound of Guy's voice. He was propped up on one elbow, watching the patterns of moonlight and shadow on her face.

'No, I . . . was too hot.' Her mouth felt dry, her voice unlike her own. 'Did I wake you?'

'It doesn't matter.' There was a pause. 'You must be stiff after your ride,' he said as the silence lengthened into tension.

'A bit.'

He hoisted himself into a sitting position and patted the side of the bed. 'Come here.'

Slowly, very slowly, Olivia went.

'Sit down,' he said quietly.

She sat, face averted, unable to look directly at him. Her heart was thudding in a slow, uneven rhythm.

He put his hands on her shoulders and began to massage the knots of tension there. 'You *are* stiff,' he said, pushing the silky hair away from the nape of her neck. His fingers moved rhythmically along her shoulders, kneading and probing, and gradually Olivia gave herself up to the sheer pleasure of uncoiling muscles and the touch of his hands, strong and sure against her skin. She was sure she could feel every whorl on his fingertips.

Her head drooped and her hair swung forward, hiding her face. He had pushed the straps of her nightdress down so that his hands could move further down her spine, and her shoulders flexed with instinctive pleasure.

'Is that better?' he asked, his voice very deep and low, and she nodded, blonde hair shimmering in the moonlight.

'Yes,' she whispered.

His fingers had stopped kneading; now only one hand slid over her back in rhythmic circles, and she lifted her head to lean back into its insistent pressure.

Her eyes were open and she stared fixedly at the band of slanting moonlight on the floor. 'Guy?'

'Yes?' His hand circled, circled, tracing deep patterns of desire on her skin.

'You remember you said...before...' She took a deep breath. 'You said you wouldn't touch me...unless I asked.'

She could feel his hand tense against her. 'I remember,' he said softly. 'There hasn't been a night since we married that I haven't remembered!'

Olivia swallowed. 'What would you say...if...if...I asked you now?' She barely breathed the words, but once they were out they seemed to bounce and reverberate around the room, and still she didn't dare look at him.

'I think...' Guy's voice was quiet, almost reflective as his hand drifted to the nape of her neck. 'I think I'd ask you why it's taken you so long,' he said eventually. He let the soft hair slide between his fingers as if to capture the moonshine spangled in the golden strands.

'I wasn't sure you'd want me,' Olivia said, but the light, tantalising brush of his fingers against her neck was making it difficult to talk.

There was a sharp intake of breath behind her, and Guy's hands tightened against her. 'Not want you?' he echoed incredulously. Bending his head, he pressed a kiss on the pure line of her shoulder, and she tilted her head back in instinctive response.

'Not want you?' he said again, letting his lips travel with long, lingering kisses from the curve of her shoulder to the arching line of her throat, the light stubble on his chin male-rough against her softness. 'Do you know how beautiful you are, Olivia? Do you know what it's been like for me, lying next to you every night with only that damned nightdress between us?' His mouth drifted up her throat, explored the soft, sensitive area beneath her earlobe until she shivered with pure pleasure.

'Why did you buy it for me?' she asked, her voice half-gasp, half-whisper. Her mind was adrift, her body abandoned to the sheer delight of Guy's warm kisses against her skin. His arms encircled her, pulling her back against the hard strength of his chest.

'Why did I buy it?' She felt him smile into her neck and his hands slid possessively over the silk. 'I just wanted to see what you looked like in it!'

Olivia tipped her head back further, turning her face to meet his as his kisses drifted on along her jawline. She could feel his heart thudding like hers as she leant back against his chest, her eyes huge and shining in the reflected light.

His lips had reached the corner of her mouth when he paused. Lifting his head to look down into her eyes, he slid his hand up her arm and gently brushed the hair back from her face.

'Are you sure you want this, Olivia?' he murmured, even as he tangled his fingers in her hair and began to drop teasing, tantalising kisses over her face.

'Yes . . . yes,' she whispered, twisting against him so that she could hold his face in her hands. 'I'm sure.'

When his lips met hers at last, it was with a dizzying explosion of relief that the hours, days, weeks of tense awareness were over. The touch and the taste and the scent of him, which had lingered so disturbingly in her mind, no longer needed to be hoarded like guilty secrets. His mouth was warm, insistent, his hands sliding in luxurious exploration over her body.

Together they sank back on to the mattress as their kisses deepened. With increasing urgency, Guy moved his hands up and down the length of Olivia's thighs, rucking up the nightdress, his murmurs of pleasure hoarse against the sleek perfection of her body. She was free at last to touch him the way she had wanted to touch him for so long. Her fingers drifted wantonly over the lean planes of his body, glorying in the gasping excitement of skin on skin, every inch explored a new delight, revelling in the discovery that Guy responded to her own touch just as she did to his.

With a muffled gasp, he rolled her beneath him again and smiled as he bent his head to kiss her lips, a long, deep kiss that left her aching with the need to feel him closer still. The silk of the night-dress whispered as he slipped it over her head, leaving her slender and quivering with exquisite anticipation beneath his gaze.

The dark desire in his eyes matched her own. Olivia was fiercely glad that his need was as obvious as her own, and she arched in frank invitation, curling her fingers in his hair in mute entreaty as he ran his hands over her golden curves, following their burning trail with his lips.

'You're beautiful,' he mumbled against her breast, his hands tightening against her. 'So perfect...'

'Guy...' Olivia moaned his name, beyond coherent thought. She could feel herself unravelling, as if every touch unwound a further layer of her protective camouflage. Sophistication, antagonism, uncertainty, jealousy, resentment... all fell away at the insistence of his lips and his hands, discovering every secret curve and dip, disentangling her from herself until she was only fire and desire in his arms.

At last, when they could bear the exquisite agony no longer, she wrapped her legs around him and cried out in release as he thrust into her, pushing her further and further, on and up in an irresistible spiral of passion until they climbed together in a final shuddering explosion of ecstasy that left them gasping, limbs entangled in wordless fulfilment.

When Olivia could open her eyes, it was with a jolt of surprise to see that the room was just the same. She felt that it should at least have been glowing in the reflected heat of their passion, but it was only very cool and very still in the white moonlight.

Guy rolled on to his back and lay without speaking, but one finger stroked the soft skin on the inside of her arm, and Olivia fell asleep, content, listening to the sound of his breathing.

The Barclinty Rodeo was one of the social occasions of the year. Everyone from two hundred miles around had come to drink beer, watch the rodeo, and, it seemed, meet Guy Richardson's new English wife.

Although assured by everyone that the rodeo was a social occasion, Olivia had hesitated over what to wear. She didn't want to be accused of being overdressed, but she simply didn't possess anything suitable. In the end she chose a vivid jade green silk dress with a very simple drop-waisted design. She had worn it to Ascot once, she remembered ruefully as she turned back the brim at the front of her straw hat. It was as close as she had ever been to a rodeo.

As soon as she arrived, she could see that her efforts to dress appropriately had backfired. True, most of the women were in dresses, but the simple elegance of her outfit stood out unmistakably, and she was certain that everyone disapproved of such an eye-catching outfit. It was so hot that she couldn't even take her hat off, so she stood feeling conspicuous and wishing she had had a career which involved wearing only dull, sensible clothes.

'It's good to know there's a woman at Willagong Creek again.'

'Yes, they sure needed a woman at Willagong Creek.'

'High time Guy Richardson found himself a woman.'

Olivia shook hands and smiled mechanically. She knew that everyone was being kind, but she couldn't help feeling a pinch of resentment. All those years of independence, of struggling to succeed, were irrelevant to these people. Was that really all she was now, just *a woman*?

Was that all she had been to Guy last night?

Out of the corner of her eye, she could see him leaning on the rail, talking to an older man and watching Darren's attempt to stay on a savagely bucking horse. He looked just as he normally did, cool, quiet, self-contained. There was nothing to suggest that this was the same man who last night had made love to her with such breathtaking passion, whose body had taken hers to the heart-stopping limits of rapture.

How could he stand there, looking just the same?

In the rush to leave for the rodeo that morning, last night had not been referred to. Guy had been fully dressed when he had shaken her awake, and he had disappeared immediately to rouse the others. By the time they had breakfasted and organised transport for everyone, it was time to go, and once out in the bright morning glare the tender intimacy of the night seemed impossibly remote. Besides, there was David, hanging over the bench seat, bemoaning the fact that he was too young to take part in the rodeo. She could hardly say anything in front of him.

'Olivia!' Guy's mother, Janet, was small and vivacious, in direct contrast to her husband, who was an older, more relaxed image of Guy. Her touch on Olivia's arm brought Olivia back to the present, and she turned to see her with a very good-looking man, whose pale skin and elegant clothes proclaimed someone who didn't belong here any more than she did. Instinctively, she gave him a smile of understanding.

'Olivia, this is James Hungerford—I thought you might like to meet a fellow Englishman! James is staying with us for a few days, so we've brought him along to see his first rodeo.'

'I'm delighted to meet you.' He had an attractive voice, though it sounded quick and rather clipped to her ears, which were accustomed to Guy's deeper, slower tones. His smile, as he shook her hand, was clearly appreciative of her vivid beauty. 'I was beginning to feel quite a foreigner, so perhaps you can give me some moral support!'

Olivia laughed. 'I know how you feel! What are you doing so far from home?'

'I'm a record producer—classics mainly. One of our orchestras has been playing at the Adelaide Festival, and I've tagged on a couple of weeks' holiday while I'm out here. A friend of mine once worked as a cook for the Richardsons, and she suggested I look them up... so here I am, seeing the outback at first hand!'

'He's coping all right,' Janet put in with an approving smile. 'Though it's not really what he's used to, is it, James?'

'It certainly isn't!' he agreed, and they all laughed at the feeling in his voice.

'You'd get used to it after a while—look at Olivia here!'

Olivia gave a wry smile. 'I don't think I'm much of an example, Janet.'

'Nonsense!' the older woman said briskly. 'Even Corky has told me how good your cooking is, and, let me tell you, compliments from Corky are hard to come by!'

The colour rushed into Olivia's cheeks. 'Did he really say that?' she said, ridiculously pleased.

'Well, he said "a bit fancy, but not bad", which is the same thing! And David told me that, although you're very boring about washing properly, you tell the most marvellous stories.' Janet paused and looked at Olivia with direct grey eyes. 'Diane would be very happy to know you were looking after him so well.'

Had Janet guessed the reason for her son's hasty marriage? Olivia met her eyes for a brief, revealing moment, then she glanced away to where David, in company with all the other little boys, was perched on the railings with the ringers.

'I hope so,' she said quietly. 'I hope so.'

'Oh, there's Alison Black...I'll see you two later.' Janet hurried off, a small, neat figure in a bright red dress.

'She's quite a lady.' James looked after her thoughtfully. 'She's the sort who can wear lipstick and lasso a cow! Do you think you'll be like that one day?'

Olivia burst out laughing. 'Why, James, what makes you think I'm not like that already?' she teased.

He pursed his lips and surveyed her slim, stylish figure. 'Just a feeling!' Then he laughed too at the absurdity of the idea of her lassoing anything.

Olivia felt rather than saw Guy straighten and turn to watch the two of them laughing together. They must look perfectly matched, she realised, both so out of place and both so *English*.

She half expected Guy to come over and join them, and when he only turned back to his companion she felt obscurely piqued. He ought to be jealous, he ought to have come hurrying over to make sure James knew she was married, he ought to have dragged her away and made her discuss cake recipes with the other women...but he was obviously more concerned with discussing the price of feed, or comparing how many points of rain they had had recently, to care that she was enjoying herself with another man.

Turning her shoulder on Guy, Olivia gave James a bright smile. 'Which orchestra have you been with?' When he told her, she nodded in delighted recognition. 'Then you must know...'

They were soon happily absorbed in talk of the music business, and for a while Olivia even forgot about Guy. It was wonderful to talk to someone who understood *her* world for a change, wonderful to hear the gossip, wonderful to meet someone to whom she wasn't just a woman at Willagong Creek. She liked James. He was good company, witty without being cruel or pretentious.

'I must say I'll be glad to get back to Townsville tomorrow,' he was saying, when they had exhausted music. 'It's been quite an eye-opener, and the Richardsons are the kindest of hosts, but I feel such an alien most of the time. I know you're married, so it must be different for you, but don't you ever wish you were back home?'

Home? Olivia took off her hat and fanned her face. It took almost an effort of memory to recall her flat in London. All she could think of was the vast sky, the silent creek and Guy's brown, sure hands on her body. She swallowed. 'Sometimes,' she said.

They stood for a while at the railings, watching the rodeo. On the far side of the dusty ring, a line of ringers sat perched on the wooden rails, identically dressed in jeans and boots and hats, and cheering good-naturedly whenever anyone fell off their horse. The bucking broncos had given way to roping a calf, and now they were trying to bring down steers by hand. James watched mystified.

'What's the point of it?' he whispered to Olivia.

Olivia had been watching Guy out of the corner of her eye. There was a certain tension about the way he stood, but he didn't look her way. 'Don't ask me!' she said, adding abruptly, 'Let's go and find a drink.'

They began to push their way through the crowd towards the beer tent. It was stifling under the canvas, and they soon escaped outside again.

'Phew!' James wiped his face with a handkerchief. 'It's worse than a sauna in there. How do you think they keep the beer so cold?'

Olivia didn't answer. Through the crowd she had caught a glimpse of Guy. He seemed to be deeply involved in a conversation with a girl in a pretty pink and white striped dress. As the girl turned slightly, Olivia realised with a blaze of incredulous jealousy that it was Robyn. A very feminine Robyn. She had flown home in the helicopter earlier that morning and now she looked transformed. She was standing just that bit too close to Guy. They matched each other almost as well as Olivia and James had done.

As if to underline the thought, Guy glanced up and saw her watching him.

Above their heads, the loudspeakers played a tinny version of a well-known folk song. Olivia could only stare back at Guy, her eyes green and hostile. He'd ignored her all day, and now there he was *fawning* over Robyn! He was probably telling her how nice she looked, pretty but not too pretty, practical but not too practical. She looked like the perfect wife for him.

Olivia turned abruptly away. What had she expected? That sleeping with Guy would change the facts? The facts were that she was the wrong wife for Guy. She loved him, but he had given no indication that he felt anything for her. There was last night, of course... but how many men would refuse when a girl begged them to make love to her?

Somehow she got through the afternoon. She chatted and smiled and shook hands and agreed that there hadn't been a woman at Willagong Creek for a long time, and all the time she was aware of Guy. Guy drinking his beer, Guy nodding seriously at some discussion, Guy watching the rodeo with narrowed, thoughtful eyes. He didn't spend his whole time with Robyn, but she always seemed to be around, part of a group, or standing casually near by at the railings.

At last the crowd began drifting away. 'Olivia, I'm going ahead to get dinner on,' said Janet, bustling up. They were to stay at Pingunaguna that night, where the Richardsons traditionally held a party after the Barclinty Rodeo. 'Could you and Guy give James a lift back?'

'Of course.' Olivia pinned her stiff smile back into place. 'I'll go and find Guy and David.'

'David's over by the horses, and I saw Guy disappearing over there with Robyn too. Tell them not to be late, won't you?'

'Is Robyn coming as well?' Olivia asked reluctantly.

'Oh, yes, the Wilsons always come. She's such a nice girl, isn't she? We've always been very fond of her. In fact, at one point we wondered if she and Guy——' As if she suddenly realised that she was being tactless, Janet broke off to glance at her watch. 'I mustn't stand here chatting! You round the others up, and I'll see you later. Don't be long!'

Olivia took off her hat and ran her fingers through her hair rather shakily. What had they wondered? That Guy would marry Robyn? She would obviously have been a more acceptable bride for him. But if that was the case, why hadn't he married her? Was he counting on the fact that his marriage to Olivia would only be for the three years he had made such a point of specifying?

Awash with jealousy and miserably conscious of how unwelcome a wife she must have been, Olivia took refuge once more in grim pride. She would *not* cry in front of all these people who disapproved of her! Biting her lip, she straightened her shoulders and wearily went in search of the others.

# CHAPTER NINE

Guy and Robyn were inspecting a horse together when they found them. Guy looked round quickly at Olivia's approach, but his expression hardened perceptibly when he saw James close behind her.

'I told your mother we'd give James a lift back,' Olivia said, summoning up all her reserves of pride to sound cool and unconcerned.

'I see.' Guy looked from her to James with a faintly contemptuous expression, then turned back to Robyn. 'What about you, Robyn? Do you want a lift?'

Olivia clenched her teeth, and forced herself to smile as Robyn glanced at her rather uncertainly. 'There's plenty of room,' she said stiffly.

'In that case, I will come,' said Robyn. 'Thanks.'

Only David seemed oblivious to the tension in the car. James, in the front seat, tried to talk to Guy, but his efforts at polite conversation met with curt, monosyllabic replies.

Olivia glared at the back of Guy's head, embarrassed by his rudeness. There was no cause for him to be unpleasant to James! When another awkward silence threatened, she launched into a brittle flow of reminiscences about a tour she had once done in Japan. James turned gratefully from the grim figure sitting beside him to listen, and Olivia forced herself to continue, even though she knew that to Guy and Robyn, effectively excluded from the conversation, she must sound unbearably pretentious. Too bad, she told herself. If they couldn't be bothered to be polite to a visitor, she wasn't going to the effort of including them!

Guy's face was like concrete as they drew up outside Pingunaguna. It was a fine old homestead, and set in a lovingly nurtured garden. Olivia couldn't help exclaiming in delight when she saw the sweep of lawn, and the bougainvillaea scrambling over the veranda. The house looked settled, cared for, an oasis of green and plenty.

Willagong Creek could look like this, she thought—but it would take longer than three years. She would never see it.

'Guy, I've put you and Olivia in your old room,' Janet called from the kitchen where she was busy chopping up salads. 'Show her where it is, then come and give me a hand with the carving, will you? David's sleeping with all the other children over in the old ringers' quarters.'

In glacial silence, Guy led Olivia along a corridor and opened the door into a small room. This was where he had grown up, she thought, looking round at the shelves of tattered books, the faded photographs of children beaming on horses—was that really Guy there? and that little boy with him looked so like David that it must be Pete!—and the collection of dusty rocks that at one time must presumably have had some significance.

When Guy still didn't speak, her gaze moved on, and stopped at the narrow bed pushed against the wall. 'We're not supposed to both sleep in that, are we?' she asked involuntarily.

Guy shut the door and threw the overnight bag on to a chair. 'You wouldn't have objected last night,' he said. 'What's the matter? Have you suddenly got fussy since you met Hungerford?'

Olivia flinched at the cool note in his voice. 'What do you mean?'

'I'd have thought it was obvious—it certainly was to everybody else at the rodeo.'

'*What* was obvious?' she asked, dangerously quiet.

'You were cosying up to him all day. Do you think nobody noticed all that giggling and whispering? Everyone was talking about how Guy Richardson's new wife could hardly keep her hands off the English bloke!' He turned away in disgust. 'I suppose he reminded you of Tim!'

Olivia's face was white with anger, her eyes a cold, clear green. 'As a matter of fact, he did! He's very good company and I like him very much!'

'As soon as I saw him, I knew he'd be just your type!' Guy said bitterly, 'And sure enough, every time I looked round, there you were, flirting with him, fluttering those eyes of yours, laughing at his jokes. What was so funny, anyway? Were you comparing notes on how *unsophisticated* everyone was?'

'You know your problem, Guy? You've just got a huge chip on your shoulder about not being sophisticated enough!' What had happened to last night's dreams? Olivia was frightened at the way the quarrel was escalating out of control, but she couldn't have held back her bitterness if she had wanted to. 'You're jealous of James because he doesn't need to jump on to a horse to prove that he's a man! He's successful and charming and amusing—all the things you'll never be!'

'You'd have liked me to be like that, wouldn't you, Olivia?' Guy sneered. 'You've wanted someone to replace Tim all along, and I was just a poor substitute. No wonder you practically fell into Hungerford's arms! A kindred spirit after all that cultural deprivation in the outback!'

'That's not true!' Olivia protested hotly. 'And I did not fall into his arms! Yes, I enjoyed talking to James, but why shouldn't I? We've got a lot in common. At least he talked to me, which is more than you did, or treat me like just another bloody woman at Willagong bloody Creek!'

'You'll never be a Willagong woman,' Guy said cruelly. 'I should have known that, as soon as you had the chance you'd go back to your old London ways, looking down your nose at anyone not as grand as you, boasting about your precious job——'

'I wasn't boasting!' she interrupted angrily.

'Oh? What was all that about Japan in the car, then? You were out to impress!'

'If you hadn't been so rude to James, I wouldn't have had to say anything! I could hardly sit there in silence while you bit his head off!'

'I don't like being patronised,' said Guy flatly.

'He wasn't being patronising,' she protested. 'He was only trying to be polite!'

'I don't want to listen to polite conversation from a man who's spent all day encouraging my wife to make an exhibition of herself.'

'I'm surprised you noticed!' Olivia's eyes blazed at the unfairness of it. 'You were so busy fawning over Robyn, I wouldn't have thought you'd have time to see what I was doing!'

'I could hardly miss what *you* were doing, Olivia, and for the record, I was not *fawning* over Robyn, as you put it. Robyn and I were merely talking about the things *we* have in common, but we managed to do it without attracting the notice of everybody else at the rodeo.'

'Of course, you've got so much in common too!' Olivia snapped. 'What a pity you didn't get round to marrying Robyn before, then you wouldn't have had to put up with me embarrassing you today!'

A muscle was beating steadily in Guy's jaw. 'Yes, it is a pity! Robyn's everything you'll never be— she doesn't flaunt herself for attention the way you do. Maybe she's not as beautiful as you, maybe she's not as sophisticated, but she's a much nicer person. She's genuine and hard-working and she wouldn't dream of making a fuss about any of the things you do. Oh, yes, you're right, it's a pity I didn't appreciate Robyn while I had the opportunity. I'm regretting it now, that's for sure. I wish I'd never agreed to marry you!'

'You can't regret it more than I do!' Olivia lashed out.

'Do you regret last night too?'

There was a pause. Olivia was breathing heavily with suppressed fury, her eyes glittering dangerously in her pale face. 'What do you think?' she retorted at last in a contemptuous voice.

Guy's eyes narrowed. 'You almost had me fooled, Olivia, you and your big blue eyes and your "please, Guy"!' He mimicked her savagely. 'Last night I really thought you wanted me, but all you wanted was a man, wasn't it? What a pity you didn't wait another day—you could have had yourself a sophisticated gentleman like you always wanted, instead of having to make do with me! Must have been tough for you, stooping so low, or did you enjoy roughing it for a change?'

White-hot fury was sliding through her veins. 'Oh, it had the charm of novelty,' she sneered, wanting to hurt him as much as he had hurt her.

'It did, did it?' In spite of her anger, the menace in his eyes had her backing nervously until she came up against the bookshelves. 'Is that what you and Hungerford were sniggering about all day? Did you tell him that you'd actually got desperate enough to try the *"cowboy technique"*?' His hands reached out to pull her against him with insulting ease. 'How long does it take for the novelty to wear off?'

'Let me go!' Olivia twisted her head frantically away, but it was too late. He swooped down on her, capturing her mouth in a savage parody of the kisses they had shared last night, forcing her lips apart, punishing her.

She fought him, but he was too strong for her, and more dangerous was the crumbling resistance within her, the insidious way her blood leapt at the remembered excitement of his touch, even as she hated what he was doing to her.

Sensing the fight seeping out of her, Guy loosened his grip to let his hands roam over the thin silk of her dress, and instinctively her body arched towards him.

She closed her eyes against the contempt in his face. She wanted to push him away, and her fingers fluttered protestingly as she struggled against uncoiling passion, but it was hopeless. Slowly, inexorably, her hands crept up his arms and round his neck to tangle in his hair and pull him closer.

With a stifled oath, he released her, pushing himself away so suddenly that she staggered and fell back against the shelves. One of the rocks, dislodged, rolled over the edge and dropped with a crack on to the wooden floor.

For a moment they just stared at each other, both breathing unevenly, then Olivia pushed the hair away from her face with a shaking hand. 'Don't you ever touch me again!' she spat at him.

'Don't worry, I won't! The Englishman's welcome to you and your *sophisticated technique*, Olivia!' He turned on his heel and walked out, banging the door shut behind him.

At first Olivia couldn't move. She stood rigid, with the shelves digging into her back, and tried to stop shaking. She hated him for the way he had reduced her so easily to writhing desire in his arms, hated herself more for having so little self-control. How could she have responded like that when he had said all those terrible things to her?

She bent to pick up the rock that had fallen off the shelf. It was dull and brown, hardly a collector's item. No wonder it had appealed to Guy, she thought bitterly. He didn't like anything different or colourful or exotic, did he?

'I wish I'd never agreed to marry you.'

Her face screwed up with the effort of not crying, she flung the rock out of the window. She only wished she could do the same thing to Guy Richardson!

When she finally emerged from the room, only the glitter in her green eyes gave any indication of the emotions seething inside her. If she had ever thought that Guy might come to love her, she knew better now. He despised her, and the only thing she had to cling on to now was pride. She would show him she didn't care!

There was a momentary silence as she stepped out on to the brightly lit veranda. She wore a clinging sleeveless dress in a stunning, simple black which emphasised the honey-coloured warmth of her skin and her slender figure. The short hemline, cut just above her knees, made her legs look longer and slimmer than ever. The effect, with her dramatic turquoise eyes and glinting hair, was dramatic.

Across the veranda, Olivia met Guy's eyes. She gave him a smile of pure provocation before turning deliberately to walk towards James, who was watching her approach with frank admiration.

'You look stunning!' he told her.

'Thank you, James.' Olivia's eyes flickered towards Guy. He wasn't even watching her! She turned abruptly back to James. 'James, can I ask you a favour?'

'Anything!'

'You mentioned you were driving to Townsville tomorrow... could I have a lift?'

'Of course.' James paused delicately. 'But won't Guy...?'

Olivia gave him a bright, innocent smile. 'He has to get back to Willagong Creek, and they're far too busy to take me shopping at the moment. I thought it might be a good opportunity to go with you, then I can get a bus back or something.' She had no real plan in mind, other than to show Guy that he couldn't speak to her like that and expect her to go home as if nothing had happened, but there was no reason to tell James that.

No one watching her bright smile as she chatted and flirted light-heartedly with the men would have guessed how close she was to tears. Guy watched her from a distance with a remote, uninterested expression that was more hurtful than open contempt. The less he responded, the more feverish her chatter grew, and the more brittle her smile until she was sure it must crack. But her control only wavered once when she found herself standing next to Guy's father, Bill. He was observing the chaotic activity round the barbecue with that air of cool detachment that was so typical of his son, and his slow smile as he turned to her was so like Guy's too that her breath caught in her throat.

'You OK, Olivia?' Bill asked, his eyes narrowing slightly at her unguarded expression.

'Oh, yes, I'm fine,' she said quickly. 'Fine.'

As he talked, she could think only that this was how Guy would look when he was old, and that she would not be there to see it. And the knife of misery twisted inside so that she gasped and fled, muttering something about 'helping Janet', terrified she would break down in front of everyone.

Behind the homestead, all was dark except for a patch of yellow light shining out from the kitchen window. Olivia leant against the wall in the shadow below and wrapped her arms about her as if she were cold.

I won't cry, I *won't*.

She stayed in the comfort of the darkness for long minutes, until with a ragged sigh she forced herself upright, only to tense as the sound of female voices in the kitchen rang through the screen netting with disastrous clarity.

'What do you think of Guy's new wife? No, not there—Janet said in the fridge.'

'Oh, yes, here it is . . . Olivia? She's a bit much, isn't she? Have you seen the way she's been carrying on with all the men this evening? And that dress! Wish I could get off with something like that!'

'She looks like she used to be a model or something,' the other girl agreed gloomily. 'Funny kind of wife for Guy, though, isn't she? I don't know what he sees in her.'

'I'd have thought it was obvious,' her friend said with some acidity. 'But I agree, it's unlike Guy to be bowled over by a beautiful face. I always thought he'd marry Robyn Wilson.'

'So did Robyn! I'll bet she's pretty sick. She'd have been a far better wife for him too. That Olivia doesn't look as if she's ever worked in her life. Did you see her hands—painted nails!'

In the darkness, Olivia's fingers curled. Her hands had been so rough after the weeks of cleaning that she had made a special effort to manicure them in expectation of the party. So much for making an effort!

'I feel sorry for Guy,' the girl went on. 'She's just not the type to settle down somewhere like Willagong Creek. What's the betting she makes his life hell?'

'I wouldn't be surprised if she left him, would you? I can't see her sticking it out here.'

'At least that would leave Guy free for Robyn.' Olivia could imagine their hopeful expressions as their voices moved away. 'I've got the bread . . . did you get the butter. . .'

Olivia stood very still in the shadows. Guy should have married Robyn. That would have made everyone happy. David would have been perfectly happy. There had been no reason to force herself on Guy. She had had to ask him to marry her, beg him to make love to her. Suddenly she burned with humiliation. Guy had made it very clear what he thought of her, but nobody else knew that he wasn't the fool he must appear, tied to an embarrassing, unsuitable wife. How many others would feel sorry for him after today?

The anger that had buoyed her up through the evening had completely evaporated. She felt only very tired. Guy was a proud man; he would hate the thought of being pitied. When she had asked James to take her to Townsville, it had been in furious reaction to Guy's contempt, but perhaps it would be better for Guy if she just left for good?

Leaving Guy would mean leaving David too. The thought tore at her heart—but how could she go back to Willagong Creek, knowing how much Guy regretted their marriage? Would David really benefit from such an unhappy situation? Did he need as much as she claimed, or was the truth that she would miss him far, far more than he would miss her?

'What are you doing standing here in the dark?' Guy appeared suddenly in front of her, and Olivia, after her first start of fright, looked quickly away, unwilling for him to see the naked longing in her eyes.

'Thinking,' she said, and then, when he made no reply, 'I'm going to Townsville tomorrow.'

'Townsville?' he repeated roughly. 'Why?'

'Why do you think?'

'Are you going with that ... with Hungerford?'

She nodded, still not looking at him. Let him think she was going with James as more than a passenger, if that was what he wanted.

There was a pause.

'Are you coming back?' Guy asked at last, as if the question had been dragged out of him.

'No.' Olivia took a deep breath. 'It's obviously not working, Guy. I just ... don't belong here.'

The anger seemed to have drained from Guy too. 'You were willing to give it a go before,' he said in a flat voice.

'That was before,' she muttered.

'I see.' He sounded oddly defeated. 'So you're running back to civilisation, is that it?'

'I think it would be better for both of us.' She clasped her hands together to stop them from shaking. 'I'm sure we can get a divorce quite easily. Then you can marry Robyn after all. She's just the kind of woman you need at Willagong Creek!'

'Yes.' Guy seemed to hear the doubtful note in his voice, for he said again, 'Yes, she is.' He half turned away. 'If you can't stand it any more, you'd better go, then. Go back to your city and your sophisticated friends, if that's what you want. I'll tell David you changed your mind.'

Olivia was mystified at the bitterness in his voice. He was the one who wanted her to go! 'It's all right, I ... I'll talk to him tomorrow.'

'He probably won't mind that much,' Guy went on callously, as if he deliberately wanted to hurt her. 'He likes Robyn.'

Olivia bit her lip. She wanted desperately to throw herself against him, to feel his arms around her, and hear him telling her he wouldn't let her go. Instead she gave a tight smile. 'I know. I'm sure he'll be fine. I'd still like to see him, of course, when I can.'

'When you can fit him in with your career?'

'I meant when it was convenient to you,' she said quietly.

'Oh.' Guy hunched a shoulder. 'Well, he'll probably go away to school quite soon. You wouldn't have had to stay much longer anyway.'

'In that case, I think we should just admit that we made a mistake and go our separate ways.' Olivia's voice trembled slightly with the effort of keeping it under control.

'It's up to you,' Guy said with a cruel lack of concern.

'I . . . I'm sorry if it puts you in an embarrassing position,' she faltered.

'What do you mean?'

'I suppose it'll look as if I walked out on you.'

'That's what you are doing, isn't it?'

'No! We've come to a mutual agreement that the arrangement we made isn't working.'

'Is that what we've done?' Guy said with an edge of sarcasm. 'Lucky I had an executive on hand to explain it to me!'

A comforting flash of anger shook Olivia. She was doing what he wanted—he might at least make things easy for her! 'I'm only trying to be civilised about this!' she snapped.

'Good for you!' He glared down at her with hostile eyes. 'But then, as you've discovered, the outback isn't a civilised enough place for you, is it, Olivia?' He turned away abruptly. 'You can have the bed. I'll find somewhere else to sleep.'

She found David early the next morning, exactly where she had expected to find him, hanging over the paddock rails and watching the horses. The party had gone on long into the night and there was no one else around.

'Can I go and stay with Brad Clark some time, Olivia?' he demanded as she joined him. 'Mrs Clark said I could.'

Olivia screwed up her eyes against the sun, and tried not to think how hard it was going to be to say goodbye to David. She had spent the night staring at the door, willing it to open, willing Guy to come in and tell her he hadn't meant any of it, but he hadn't come, and in the end she accepted that he must want her to leave after all. After that, there was no going back. There was only David to see.

'Who's Brad?' she asked. Anything to put off having to tell him.

'He's my friend. He's a year and two months older than me. I met him at the rodeo yesterday.'

'If Mrs Clark says you can stay, I'm sure it'll be all right.'

'Good.' Pleased at not meeting the expected opposition, David turned back to the horses.

'Would you like to go back with Brad today—if Mrs Clark doesn't mind?'

'OK.' David looked at her, puzzled. 'Why?'

'Oh, I . . . the thing is . . .' she floundered. In the paddock, the horses grazed peacefully, flicking their tails against the flies. 'The thing is, David, I'm going to Townsville today.'

'When are you coming back?'

There was a pause. 'I'm not coming back,' she said.

David's face went very still. He climbed down off the railings. 'Is it because of me?'

'No!' Olivia said quickly. 'It's because of me—and Guy.'

'I overheard somebody at the rodeo saying that you probably married Guy because of "the kid".' He looked down at his feet. 'That's me, isn't it? Is that why you got married?'

Olivia's heart cracked as she looked down at his bent head. He deserved honesty at least. 'Yes,' she said gently, 'you're the reason we got married, but you're not the reason I'm going, I promise you, David.' She turned to lean her back against the rails, and tried to think of the words to explain. 'You don't know what it's like to be in love, so you might not understand. I'm in love with Guy, David, but he's not in love with me, and it makes it very . . . hard. He'd rather be married to someone else, you see. Someone who'd be a better wife for him than me. Someone who'd probably be a better mother for you.' She hesitated. 'I'd ask you if you wanted to come with me, David, but I know how much you love Willagong Creek, and I haven't got another home to offer you yet. I don't want you to think that I don't care for you very, very much.'

David was still looking at the ground. His lower lip was stuck out and his small face was fierce with concentration. Olivia swallowed. She was trying hard not to cry herself.

'I'm only going because I think it would be better for you as well as for Guy if I went,' she went on, desperate for him to understand. 'This way you'll all be much happier, I promise. But as soon as I have somewhere to stay, you can come and see me as often as you want...OK?'

There was a long pause. At last David managed a nod, and then, abruptly, he turned and ran away from her as if she had struck him.

Last night, reliving the terrible scenes with Guy, Olivia had been unable to cry, but now she just stood for long minutes and let the tears pour noiselessly down her face, awash with black despair, and the terrible pain of having seen the two people she loved most in the world turn away from her.

'Olivia? Is everything all right?'

She hadn't heard Janet come up behind her, and turned quickly to face the paddock, surreptitiously brushing the tears from her cheeks. Unable to speak, she nodded.

Janet came to stand beside her and tactfully looked out at the horses. 'James is about to leave. He said you wanted to go into Townsville with him—is that right?'

Olivia nodded again.

'It's not my business, I know, but have you and Guy had an argument? He wouldn't say anything to me this morning. He just looked through me and walked off towards the horizon.' Janet shook her head. 'He was always like that when he was upset. Even when he was a very little boy, he used to bottle things up.'

'He wasn't bottling things up yesterday!' Olivia burst out, betrayed into a choking sob.

'So you have had an argument!' Janet shook her head, but her tolerant smile faded when she saw the ravaged face Olivia turned to her. The distraught girl before her bore little resemblance to the alarmingly sophisticated woman Guy had introduced yesterday. 'My dear,' she said with impulsive sympathy, 'what on earth's the matter?'

'Everything!' Olivia gave in and burst into tears. Collapsing on to the rail, she pillowed her face in her arms and cried as if her heart was breaking.

Concerned, Janet patted her shoulder. 'Now, now, things can't be that bad!'

'They are! Guy hates me, and I've made David cry, and I love him so much—David, I mean—and now I've got to go away and I'll probably never see him again,' Olivia sobbed incoherently.

'But why do you have to go away?'

'Guy wants to m-marry Robyn.'

Janet's eyebrows lifted in surprise. 'But he's married to you!'

'We only got married for David's sake,' Olivia explained, between sobs. 'But it hasn't worked out. Guy didn't really want to get married in the first place. I'm never going to fit in here. We're going to get a divorce so Guy can marry Robyn. You were right, Guy should have married her.'

'Did I say that?' Janet asked, startled.

'You said you'd always thought they'd get married, or something like that.'

Janet looked troubled. 'We might have thought that, Olivia, but it doesn't mean anything. If he'd wanted to marry Robyn, he could have married her years ago, but he didn't, he married you. I've known Guy longer than anyone, Olivia, and, ever since he was a baby, I've never once known him do anything he didn't want to do!'

'Well, he wants me to leave now! He doesn't love me.' Olivia gave a shuddering sigh and wiped her cheeks with the back of her hand. 'And I don't love him,' she added defiantly. 'I'm crying because of David, not because of Guy.'

'And I suppose he hasn't gone off looking as if he's been punched in the stomach because of you either?'

'He's probably just gone to look at some cows,' Olivia said bitterly.

Janet half smiled. 'I think the stock is the last thing on his mind right now.' She laid her hand firmly on Olivia's shoulder. 'These men aren't used to talking about their feelings, Olivia, but it doesn't mean they don't feel the same as anyone else.' When Olivia looked stubbornly unconvinced, Janet went on, 'You know, when I met you yesterday, I thought you were quite the wrong sort of wife for Guy. I suspected David might have had something to do with it, and quite frankly I didn't like the idea that you might have persuaded Guy into a loveless marriage. But I changed my mind when I saw the look in his eyes this morning. He wouldn't look like that unless he felt very strongly about something, and I think that something is you.'

Olivia was staring out into the paddock, but Janet was sure that she had her full attention. 'Guy's a very self-contained person. He needed someone to shake him off balance, to make him less detached. A girl like Robyn would have made him a suitable wife, sure, but he needs someone who can make him really...*feel*.'

'I make him feel the wrong things, though!' Olivia burst out. 'You didn't hear what he said to me last night. We had a terrible argument.'

'Olivia, Guy wouldn't be arguing if he didn't care more than he wants to admit, even to himself. Even as a boy, he never argued. He just went off and quietly did exactly as he wanted! With you he's behaving uncharacteristically—that's a good sign.'

'But so much of what he said is right!' Janet's words had lit a spark of hope in Olivia's heart, but now she slumped back into despair. 'I'm not the right kind of wife for him. I just don't belong here.'

'You belong with the man you love,' Janet said firmly. 'And you do love Guy, don't you, Olivia?'

Olivia turned her head to meet Janet's clear gaze. 'Yes,' she whispered. 'Oh, yes, I do.'

'Well, in my book that makes you the right kind of wife for Guy. It doesn't matter that you can't lasso a steer or brand a calf. What matters is what you feel for Guy.'

'Do you really think he might love me?' Olivia asked, hardly daring to hope again.

'He's showing every sign of it,' Janet said in a dry voice. 'He just might not know it yet.'

'So you think I should stay after all?'

Janet wriggled her nose thoughtfully. 'No-o,' she said at last. 'It wouldn't do him any harm to realise what he stands to lose, and you could probably do with some time to yourself. I don't suppose there's been much time at Willagong Creek to think things through properly. Why don't you go with James as you arranged and spend a few days in Townsville? I'll make sure Guy knows where to find you. And don't worry about David. I'll keep him here until you and Guy have sorted yourselves out.'

# CHAPTER TEN

IN SPITE of Janet's encouragement, it took all Olivia's control to get into the car and drive away from Guy and David without saying goodbye.

'You will tell Guy where I am?' she begged as she clung to Janet.

'Of course I will.'

'And David? You'll look after him?'

'I promise.' Janet shook her head in resignation. 'Don't worry!' She opened the car door. 'Go on, in you get!' Closing the door on Olivia, she bent to say a last goodbye through the open window. 'You're doing the right thing,' she reassured her.

*Was* she? Olivia spent the long hours in the car wondering if Guy would follow her. It always happened in stories. As soon as the hero found that his heroine had gone, he leapt on his white charger and set off in hot pursuit. The little plane wasn't quite as romantic as a white charger, but it would be quicker. If he wanted to, Guy could be in Townsville tonight...

But what if he didn't come? As the long miles passed, the hope that Janet had encouraged began to seem less and less realistic. Olivia replayed the arguments with Guy again and again in her mind, and each time the remembrance of bitterness grew.

'I wish I'd never agreed to marry you.'

174

'You'll never be a Willagong woman.'

Janet might be wrong. Guy might not come.

It was a long, silent drive to Townsville. Much to her relief, after a glance at her preoccupied face, James refrained from small talk. Only when he lifted her overnight bag out of the car outside the hotel did he say hesitantly, 'I'm supposed to be flying to Sydney tomorrow, but if there's anything at all I can do for you...'

Olivia summoned a smile. 'It's sweet of you, James, but I'll be fine—really.'

'What about dinner tonight?'

She looked at him as if for the first time. He was good-looking, charming, good company. Only a few weeks ago she would have been delighted to have spent an evening with him. But a vision of Guy rose before her—Guy tipping back his hat, Guy looking up from his work with those eyes that could reach inside her and squeeze her heart, Guy swinging himself on to his horse, Guy smiling, Guy's hands against her skin—and a wave of longing shook her, so strong that she almost cried out with disappointment when the vision faded and it was only James standing before her.

'I'd rather be on my own, James,' she admitted at last. 'But thank you—and thank you for the lift too. I'm sorry I wasn't much company.'

'That's all right—I understand.' James leant forward and kissed her cheek. 'I hope everything works out for you, Olivia.'

I hope so too, Olivia thought forlornly, watching him drive away.

She turned and walked into the hotel. This was where she had first met Guy. It was one of the best hotels in Townsville, modern, comfortable, luxurious even. She had always enjoyed staying in places like these, but now the subtle lighting and elegant anonymity crowded in on her, suffocating her.

Sliding open the glass door, she stepped out on to the balcony of her room and gazed down at the street below her. At Willagong Creek she had longed to be back in a familiar city environment; now she was here she felt cramped and unsettled. Could she really have changed so much in such a short time?

The evening stretched interminably as she waited and hoped for a knock on the door, but by eleven o'clock she accepted that Guy wouldn't come, at least not that night. Had he gone back to Willagong Creek after all? It would be very dark and still there now. He would be lying alone in the big bed. Was he thinking about her? Was he missing her? Why didn't he come? She fell asleep at last and dreamt of open horizons and bright light and a slow, slow smile.

She spent the next day hanging around the hotel, hating herself for still hoping against hope that Guy might appear, and terrified to go too far in case she missed him. She sat in the foyer where she had first seen him, and every time a tall, lean figure in a hat came in her heart would leap, then thud back into place with sickening disappointment.

At last she began to get angry. Guy obviously wasn't coming. He had managed perfectly well without her before. He didn't need her, he didn't want her, so why was she sitting here waiting for him? It was time to face the truth. She would go away for a few days, to one of the islands on the Barrier Reef, and decide how she was going to get through the rest of her life without him.

The coral island she chose was idyllic, but she was blind to the beauty of white sandy beaches and palm-fringed skies. Instead she stared out at the sea and thought about the dry, red Willagong dust and how empty the future seemed.

By the time she left the Reef, her decision was made. London was too far away from David, so somehow she must stay in Australia. If she could get a job, find somewhere to live, he could at least come and stay with her sometimes. Eventually she might even be able to meet Guy and they could make light of their disastrous attempt at marriage. Maybe.

For now, a job was a priority. Olivia threw herself into making plans. It took her mind off the dull ache of unhappiness and the terrible feeling that she was hurtling in completely the wrong direction. Sydney seemed the obvious place to find someone who could use her experience, and as soon as she arrived back in Townsville, desperate to commit herself before she changed her mind, she booked herself a ticket for the following morning. Guy wasn't coming for her, so she might as well go.

But she couldn't go without finding out if David was all right. Dialling the Pingunaguna number, she finally got through to Janet. It was a terrible line, and Olivia had to shout to make herself understood above the crackle of static.

'Where have you been?' Janet yelled when she had established who it was.

'Out on the Reef,' Olivia shouted back. 'I'm flying to Sydney tomorrow morning.'

'Going where?'

'Sydney!' Olivia was feeling hoarse already.

'Sydney? But why?'

'Well . . .' Olivia swallowed. 'There doesn't seem much point in waiting for Guy to turn up.' Her voice wobbled treacherously and she took a steadying breath. 'I've decided to try and find a job—Sydney seems a good place to start.'

'Look, Olivia, I don't think . . .' The line faded and Janet's voice was drowned out by static.

Olivia shook the receiver, in panic lest she lose her only link to Willagong Creek. 'Hello! Hello! Janet, are you there?'

'I said I don't think you should go, not yet,' Janet shouted. 'Can't you just wait a few days?'

'No, I . . . I've made up my mind. My flight's at nine o'clock, and I'm going to be on it. Guy could have found me if he'd wanted to, Janet. He's made it pretty clear that I'm not that important, so I'm just going to have to get on with my own life.' Janet started to say something, but Olivia interrupted her. 'I really just wanted to know how David is.'

'He's fine.' The line faded again and then came back with a deafening whine. 'Are you sure you're doing the right thing, Olivia?' Janet asked, concerned.

'I don't see what else I can do,' Olivia said wearily.

An unintelligible crackle answered her. 'What?' she bellowed.

Another crackle, but this time she caught the word 'Guy'. Olivia bit her lip in frustration. 'I'm sorry, Janet, I can't hear you,' she shouted when they had tried for a third time. 'I'll have to go. And Janet, will you ... will you give my love to David?'

She hoped Janet had heard her. Slowly she replaced the receiver. Her last faint hope, that Janet might have had some message from Guy, had gone. Now she really would have to go.

Olivia stood in the airport terminal, fingering her boarding-card. The flight had been announced, and already a queue was forming, shuffling inexorably towards the gate.

This, then, was it. Now that the moment had arrived, Olivia was conscious of an overwhelming urge to run back outside, back to Willagong Creek, back to Guy. But of course she couldn't. David and Guy were fine without her. She would have to get on the plane and leave them behind.

The boarding-card was crumpled beyond recognition. She straightened it out as best she could, and headed resolutely for the queue.

The other passengers had paused and were looking towards the entrance to the departure lounge, where some kind of altercation seemed to be taking place. Incuriously, she turned to see what all the fuss was about—and froze with incredulous shock.

Guy was standing, arguing heatedly with a uniformed airline official who was barring his path into the lounge. 'I *know* I haven't got a boarding-pass! Just let me have a look, will you? I just need to see if she's——'

He broke off as he caught sight of Olivia over the official's shoulder. She was wearing the jade-green dress she had worn on that disastrous day at the rodeo, standing stock still, oblivious to the people around her who, disappointed that there wasn't going to be more of a scene, were jostling back into the queue.

As if everything were happening in slow motion, she saw Guy push the official's arm aside and walk deliberately towards her through the crowds. They might have been the only two people in the building.

Hit by the sudden conviction that it was just a cruel hallucination, Olivia squeezed her eyes shut. She couldn't bear it not to be him. Let him be real, she prayed. Let it be Guy.

When she opened them, he was still walking towards her. She wanted to smile, to run and meet him halfway, but her body refused to respond, and in the end she could only stand foolishly, watching his unhurried progress with dazed blue eyes.

When at last he stood in front of her, he let his breath out in a long sigh of relief, as if he had feared she might turn and run. 'Olivia,' he said, then stopped, unable to go on. He was wearing jeans and a dull green work shirt. There was a tear in his sleeve, just where it was rolled up to his elbow, and Olivia found herself clutching at the detail as if it was the only proof that he was really there.

A stout, harassed-looking official was bearing down on them. 'Look, mate, the bloke over there told you you weren't allowed in here without a boarding-card. You'll have to leave—and the young lady'll have to board now. You should have said your goodbyes outside.'

Guy ignored him. 'Where are you going?' he demanded.

'Sydney,' she whispered. It was the first thing she had said.

'What for?'

'I need a job.'

There was a pause. 'There's a job for you at Willagong Creek.'

Olivia swallowed. 'What about Robyn?' She couldn't tear her eyes off him, and looking down into her face, Guy seemed suddenly to relax.

'I decided that she wasn't suitable for the position after all.'

'Of course she's suitable!' Olivia burst out in sudden bitterness.

The last of the passengers had disappeared on to the plane by now and the airline official sighed. 'Look, miss, are you getting on this flight or not?'

Robyn was all the reasons she was leaving. 'I . . . I have to go now, Guy.' Olivia made as if to turn away, but he reached out and grasped her wrist to stop her.

They both stared down at his tight, angry grip, then he slowly released her. He looked into her eyes and his voice was very quiet when he spoke. 'Don't go,' he said. 'Please stay.'

'Well?' The official put his hands on his hips. 'Are you coming or not?'

Olivia was still staring into Guy's eyes and the expression she read there made her shake her head slowly. 'No,' she said, 'I'm not going.'

'You can close the gate, Pete,' the official called wearily over to his colleague, who was muttering into his walkie-talkie about the delay. 'The lady's decided to stay after all.'

Guy and Olivia hardly heard him. The slow smile that started in Guy's eyes grew and grew as he realised that Olivia was not, after all, going to run on to the plane, and, as he smiled, Olivia, still dazed by her sudden reprieve, could only smile wordlessly back at him.

'Come on,' he said, taking her hand. 'We can't talk here.'

He led her to the other side of the airport, to where the familiar little red and white plane was parked next to the other light aircraft on a quiet corner of the runway. They seemed to shimmer in the heat bouncing off the tarmac, and the metal wings flashed in the sun. Olivia was content to walk in silence. All she needed to know for now was that Guy was there beside her.

There were some boxes of tinned peaches stacked in the shade of a hut. They sat and watched a small plane scoot down the runway, propeller blurring, and lift itself effortlessly into the vibrant blue of the sky. When it was no more than a dot in the distance, Guy said, as if to himself, 'I nearly missed you.' He held her hand tightly, reassuring himself that she was still there.

'Did Janet tell you where I was?'

He nodded. 'The day you left—I'll never forget it—I came back and she told me you'd gone with James Hungerford.' He half smiled. 'I wanted to kill him! I was beside myself with jealousy and anger, furious with him, with you, with my mother for not locking you up and refusing to let you go. She told me I'd been a fool and that I should go after you, but I was too bitter, too hurt. I went back to Willagong Creek determined that I never wanted to see you again.' He paused, his eyes still on the tiny plane in the distance. 'I managed to hold out for a day. In the end, I swallowed my pride and flew to Townsville to look for you, but you'd gone. I tried the hotel where we met, and they said you'd checked out. All day I just wandered round the town, hoping against hope that I'd see you, but it wasn't any good. I had to go back and try and tell myself that it was all for the best, that you'd never be happy in the outback.'

He turned slowly to look at her. 'That was the longest week of my life, Olivia. I was in black despair until my mother managed to get a radio message to me first thing this morning. All she said was that your plane left at nine. I came straight away, but I was nearly too late. I'd been running round the terminal trying to find you. When I saw you standing there, I felt...' His voice trailed off as he searched for the right words. 'I can't tell you how I felt,' he admitted eventually.

Gently, Olivia laid the back of her hand against his cheek. 'You don't need to explain,' she said. 'I know.'

'Do you, Olivia?' Guy asked, his voice very deep. 'Do you know what it feels like to love someone so much that it hurts just to look at them? To fall hopelessly in love with the very opposite of what you've always wanted?' He brought his hand up to cover hers. 'Do you know what it's like to think that you've lost them because you're too scared to admit it?'

'Yes,' she said simply, 'I know how all that feels. I love you, Guy. I think I've loved you from the beginning.'

For a long moment he searched her face with his eyes, as if hardly daring to believe what she was saying, then he drew her towards him for a kiss of such fierce possessiveness that Olivia felt as if she would dissolve with happiness.

'I'm sorry for those things I said to you,' he said at last, burying his face against the softness of her hair. 'I didn't mean any of it. I never wanted to marry Robyn.'

'Even though she's so suitable?' Olivia teased, safely held against him.

'I pretended I'd never had time to find a suitable wife, but it wasn't true. There were lots of suitable girls if I'd wanted them, but I didn't. Deep down I wanted a girl like the one Diane used to show me

photos of.' Guy kissed her ear, and she could feel
him smiling. 'I thought you were the most beautiful girl I'd ever seen, but I knew you were out of
my reach. Diane was always saying how glamorous
and successful you were. She'd read out bits of your
letters, and it sounded as if you were always out
on the town with some man. I knew that even if I
ever met you you would never be interested in me.
I suppose I convinced myself I disliked you as a
sort of self-defence.

'And then when you came, and I did meet you,
you were just as I'd always imagined you. When
you asked me to marry you, I couldn't believe it.
This beautiful girl, suddenly asking if she could
stay.' He paused again, tightening his arms about
her. 'I think you were right about me having a chip
on my shoulder. I wanted you desperately, but you
were such a city girl. I thought that if you'd been
in love with Tim—and you made a point of telling
me how different he was—you'd sneer at the idea
of a country boy like me, so I pretended not to
care. I was afraid to touch you, afraid I'd lose
control if I did and that you'd despise me for it.

'But I kept getting glimpses of a different Olivia
from the one I was nervous of. I saw the way you
were with David, the way you battled with the dust
every day. The more I saw of you, the more I loved
you, and I thought that perhaps I could *try*. That's
why I bought you the nightdress. I was going to
make my big move that night, but when I came in,
you were reading Tim's letter and suddenly it

seemed as if you were still in love with him. I felt
as if I'd been kicked in the stomach!'

'I don't think I was ever really in love with Tim,'
Olivia said reflectively, running her hand over Guy's
arm. 'I thought you resented me for not being the
kind of wife you needed at Willagong Creek.'

Guy tilted her face up to his. 'You're *not* the right
kind of wife,' he said. 'I needed a strong, practical
wife, not a girl who wears high heels and faints at
the sight of blood, but when you'd gone nothing
seemed worth doing any more. The ringers all sat
around remembering your cooking, and looking at
me as if I was some kind of tyrant for driving you
away. When I went down to the creek, it wasn't
peaceful any more, it was just empty. I kept
expecting to see you, painting your nails or shaking
back your hair or wrinkling up your nose in that
fastidious little way you have. Then I'd remember
that you'd gone, and that you weren't coming back.
That's when I realised I didn't need a suitable wife
at all. I needed *you*.' He bent his head to kiss her
again.

'To think I was so jealous of Robyn!' Olivia
sighed happily.

'It's nothing to how I felt seeing you with James
Hungerford at the rodeo! You seemed so pleased
to see him, and I thought he was reminding you of
everything you'd been missing about your old life.
I was convinced you wished you'd never asked me
to make love to you.'

'I would never wish that, Guy,' Olivia said, her
mouth curved in a reminiscent smile. 'And now that

I know that you love me I'll be able to ask you again and again!'

Guy's smile sent shivers of pure desire down her spine. 'Think I can't ask for myself?'

'Well,' she said virtuously, 'I've had to do all the asking so far!'

'Yes, you have.' His face was serious as he took her face in his hands and looked deep into her eyes. 'It's my turn to ask now. Will you marry me, Olivia?'

'We're already married,' she pointed out.

'We're married for the wrong reasons, and we're only married for three years. I'm asking you to marry me because you love me. This time there'll be no let-out clauses when David goes to school. I'm asking you to marry me for ever. Will you?'

Olivia's eyes were shining as she nodded. 'Yes,' she said simply, and pulled his head down to hers for a kiss which told him more than words could ever do.

'Now that we're properly married, I should take you on a proper honeymoon,' Guy said later. 'David's longing to see you again—he missed you almost as much as I did—but he'll be all right with my mother for another few days.' He brushed the hair away from Olivia's face with tender fingers. 'Well? Where would you like to go?'

She thought. They could go out to the Barrier Reef again, or down to one of the cities—Sydney, or Adelaide perhaps. Or Bali. There were plenty of exotic, sophisticated places she would like.

And there was a rough, ramshackle, sunburnt place under the huge outback sky, where the gums were silhouetted against the light and the silence settled on a dusty homestead. A place where there were no luxuries, none of the comforts she had used to think so essential, only a small boy and a lean, brown man with a slow smile.

'I'd like to go to Willagong Creek,' she said.

# ® HARLEQUIN ROMANCE®

**Harlequin Romance
has love in
store for you!**

Don't miss next
month's title in

## THE BRIDAL COLLECTION

## A WHOLESALE ARRANGEMENT
### by Day Leclaire

**THE BRIDE** *needed* the Groom.
**THE GROOM** *wanted* the Bride.
**BUT THE WEDDING** was *more* than
a convenient solution!

Available this month in
The Bridal Collection
Only Make-Believe
by Bethany Campbell
Harlequin Romance #3230

Available wherever Harlequin books are sold.

WED-8

**HARLEQUIN ROMANCE®**

Some people have the spirit
of Christmas all year round...

People like Blake Connors
and Karin Palmer.

Meet them—and love them!—in
Eva Rutland's
ALWAYS CHRISTMAS.

Harlequin Romance #3240
Available in December wherever
Harlequin books are sold.

HRHX

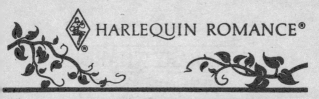

# HARLEQUIN ROMANCE®

After her father's heart attack, Stephanie Bloomfield comes home to Orchard Valley, Oregon, to be with him and with her sisters.

*Orchard Valley*

Steffie learns that many things have changed in her absence—but not her feelings for journalist Charles Tomaselli. He was the reason she left Orchard Valley. Now, three years later, will he give her a reason to stay?

"The Orchard Valley trilogy features three delightful, spirited sisters and a trio of equally fascinating men. The stories are rich with the romance, warmth of heart and humor readers expect, and invariably receive, from Debbie Macomber."

—Linda Lael Miller

Don't miss the Orchard Valley trilogy by Debbie Macomber:

VALERIE   Harlequin Romance #3232 (November 1992)
STEPHANIE   Harlequin Romance #3239 (December 1992)
NORAH   Harlequin Romance #3244 (January 1993)

Look for the special cover flash on each book!

Available wherever Harlequin books are sold.   ORC-2

HARLEQUIN ◆ PRESENTS®

## BARBARY WHARF

### Home to the *Sentinel*
### Home to passion, heartache and love

*Charlotte Lamb*

The BARBARY WHARF six-book saga continues with
Book Three, TOO CLOSE FOR COMFORT. Esteban
Sebastian is the *Sentinel*'s marketing director *and* the
company heartthrob. But beautiful Irena Olivero wants
nothing to do with him—he's always too close for comfort.

And don't forget media tycoon Nick Caspian and his
adversary Gina Tyrrell. Their never-ending arguments are
legendary—but is it possible that things are not quite what
they seem?

TOO CLOSE FOR COMFORT (Harlequin Presents
#1513) available in December.